THE FREEDOM ARMY

To escape war, humanity takes a drug that kills emotion. But insurgents, including the returning astronauts from a mission to Mars, refuse to take the drug and wage an armed rebellion. The Freedom Army, which includes the Physicist Burges, is beseiged in a bunker. However, Burges constructs a gateway to another dimension — an alternate existence — and ex space pilot Lanson leads their escape ... only to face an alternate world where humanity is enslaved by a toad-like alien race, the Zytlen!

E. C. TUBB

THE FREEDOM ARMY

Complete and Unabridged

LINFORD
Leicester

First published in Great Britain

First Linford Edition
published 2009

British Library CIP Data

Tubb, E. C.
  The freedom army
  1. Suspense fiction.
  2. Large type books.
  I. Title
  823.9′12–dc22

ISBN 978–1–84782–639–8

Published by
F. A. Thorpe (Publishing)
Anstey, Leicestershire

Set by Words & Graphics Ltd.
Anstey, Leicestershire
Printed and bound in Great Britain by
T. J. International Ltd., Padstow, Cornwall

This book is printed on acid-free paper

1

De Bracy's Drug

The walls were of bare concrete, mottled with damp and stained with time. A pattern of fine cracks marred the once smooth surface, and little heaps of dust glinting with specks of silicon and grey with cadmium lay beneath them. Blue light painted the walls with a harsh, shadowless glare, and the soft whine of the air purifiers complemented the strident chatter of the geigers.

From time to time the walls shook a little, the tiny cracks widening, thin trails of dust sifting from them to join the waiting piles on the floor. Coinciding with the tremors, the geigers chattered a little louder, a little more eagerly, then died as the walls stilled again.

'How much longer, Lanson?' A man swung from his seat before a complex instrument panel and looked worriedly at the other occupant of the chamber.

Lanson shrugged. 'Depends on the structure, but it can't be very long now.' He stared at a wall and idly ran his fingers along one of the widening cracks. 'They built well,' he murmured.

'Not well enough!'

'As well as they could,' Lanson said with quiet reproach. He was a tall man, with a supple, slender build and an easy carriage betraying hidden strength. His skin was pale from lack of sunlight, and his thick, black hair clung damply to his high forehead. Faint lines of good humour saved the firm mouth from cruelty, and his eyes were as black as space.

He moved restlessly about the instrument-lined chamber, his black uniform with the blazing gold insignia rumpled and creased. Dark patches beneath his eyes told of lost sleep.

'Regret it, Bender?'

'No. Not yet at any rate, but I probably will.' Bender rested his head in his hands, his blond hair giving him a startling boyish appearance. 'If we could only fight back!'

The walls shook and powder spilled from the cracks. The geiger counters chattered as radioactivity seeped in from the exploding bombs, then faded back into their steady murmur.

'How they must hate us,' muttered Bender.

'They have reason to, but I don't think that they are capable of hate. We are an obstacle, therefore they must destroy us.' Lanson smiled tightly. 'It is as simple as that.'

'Like a man stepping on an ant.' Bender glared at his dead instruments. 'We mean nothing to them one way or the other, but because they wanted Earth, and wanted it their way, we have to die.' He spun from his seat, eyes glinting strangely in the blue lighting. 'Is there nothing we can do?'

'Nothing.' Lanson was very calm. 'We knew what the end would be. We chose to be different from the majority, and now we pay the price of individuality. Personally, I wouldn't have had it otherwise.'

'I still can't understand it,' muttered Bender. 'It happened so suddenly. When we left on the Mars flight, Earth was normal, when we returned — ' He looked helplessly at Lanson.

'The flight to Mars and back took more than three years, and a lot can happen in that time.' Lanson fumbled in his tunic pocket for cigarettes, lit one, and sent blue smoke wreathing across the chamber. 'We should have expected it, but how could we guess? People had reached their breaking point, they had sickened of the constant fear of potential war, starvation and poverty. De Bracy's method offered them security, utter and final security, and they took it. Can we blame them?

'Not all took it. Some held out, more than we knew. This wasn't the only strongpoint to be defended.'

'Maybe we were the ones that were wrong?' Bender sounded very tired. 'De Bracy offered something man has searched for since time began. Why should we be the only ones to refuse it?'

Lanson snorted and stamped on the butt of his cigarette. 'De Bracy solved a problem in the only way such problems can be solved, by eliminating the problem, not by finding a solution. It is the wrong thing. You can't cure cancer by killing everyone who has cancer. They couldn't cure smallpox that way, and they certainly couldn't cure foot and mouth disease, they tried it long enough. No. De Bracy was an idealist, and his death only served to make him a martyr. He knew that the cause of man's unhappiness lay in unstable emotions; hate, fear, greed, desire, envy, all fought with his intellect and brought the entire race to the verge of insanity. De Bracy thought that he had discovered a remedy.'

'What a remedy,' Bender snarled. 'I had a girl when I left for Mars. A normal, warm-blooded human creature, and we'd intended to marry on my return. I came back to find a zombie!'

'I know,' agreed Lanson. 'I know only too well.' He sighed and his eyes glazed as he stared into the past. 'De Bracy perfected a drug which effectively killed all emotion. A man could no longer feel the stirrings of hate or fear. A woman no longer felt desire or love. De Bracy turned a warm, impulsive human race into a collection of robot-like intelligences. Logic ruled. Cold, inhuman logic, and logic decided that all must be the same.'

The walls shook, fragments of concrete flaking from the roof and buttresses. The lights flickered, went out, then burned again with a dull glow. The chattering of the geigers echoed through the chamber.

'We'd better go below,' decided Lanson. 'This chamber will be the first to be blasted, and radioactivity is too high for safety as it is.'

'Burges won't like it! He asked me to leave him alone for as long as possible.'

'Burges?' Lanson frowned then smiled apologetically. 'The physicist, I'd forgotten him. What's he doing?'

'Working on something, he wouldn't tell me what.' Bender straightened himself, flinching at a fresh tremor of the walls. 'Shall we go?' He raised a trap door under their feet. Lanson shrugged and followed him down. Concrete rattled on the closing hatch.

A small man blinked at them as they edged their way past a mass of electronic equipment. He stood at a metal bench intent on soldering a complex mass of wires to a metal and plastic frame. He ignored Bender's greeting.

'Funny people these scientists,' Bender murmured to Lanson. 'His life can be measured in hours, and yet he works at something which will be destroyed with him.'

'Emotion versus logic,' explained Lanson. 'If we'd have taken De Bracy's drug, we would have shot ourselves hours ago, after we had fired the last torpedo at the attacking ships.'

'What made you refuse the drug?' Bender looked at his tall companion curiously. 'You had no girl friend, no real reason for refusing. You could have had a high position with the space fleet, and yet you refused. Why?'

'I had my reasons.' Lanson stretched his lithe figure. 'Maybe it's because I have a weakness for lost causes, maybe for some other reason, but I couldn't take the drug.' He smiled at Bender's expression. 'There will always be the obstinate ones, the stubborn ones, the just plain awkward. I've never liked doing what the mob did, perhaps that is why I went to space. Earth had grown dull to a man with a craze for adventure, and I've always wanted to see what lay over the next hill. Space offered me a way out, and I pulled every string I could to get command of the Mars flight.

'What had I to lose? A safe, snug little life, doing what I was told to do, or what cold logic forced me to do. Never feeling the surging of hate, triumph, exultation at doing a good job, and doing it well. Just spiritual death.' For a moment his mobile face contorted, the lines around his mouth deepening, stamping his features with cruelty.

'I hate De Bracy for what he did to mankind. They're out there, waiting, calmly bombing this strongpoint to atomic dust, merely because we refused to join the crowd. When I joined the insurgents I knew what the end must be, yet I would join again. Sabotage failed, frontal attack failed, research for an anti-serum failed. All we could do was to run to these strongpoints, relics of an age when men hated each other and prepared for war, and here we made our last stand.'

'Their losses were high.' Bender had a trace of satisfaction in his voice. 'It would have been wiser for them to have left us alone.'

'That is the one thing they couldn't do. They are idealists, and an idealist is so sure that he is right, and so certain that what he does is good for all, that he will do it if he has to kill you in the attempt.' Lanson sighed and stared at his hands.

'There is another reason why they must kill us. They are not quite certain that what they have done is the right thing to do. For their own peace of mind they cannot allow any untreated persons liberty, to do so would give them a unit of comparison, and the treatment is irrevocable. They dare not be proved wrong.'

The walls quivered, flakes of concrete falling to the dusty floor. The lights flickered then steadied to their normal blue glow. Bender shuddered.

'Time's almost up,' he said with forced cheerfulness.

'They are being logical,' mused Lanson. 'They are probably using this strongpoint as a practice target. Even fifty feet of silicon-cadmium reinforced concrete with five feet of lead cushion, wouldn't stand up to normal atomic bombs this long. They are using small fission missiles, and they are taking their time.'

'Damn them!' Bender glared at the roof, now misty with coiling dust. His too handsome face twisted, the thick blond curls damp against his forehead. 'Do they have to play with us like this?'

'Steady, Bender!' warned Lanson. He gripped the younger man's arm. 'Don't crack now. We've had our fun, now it's their turn.'

A muttered curse from the direction of the bench followed by a banging of tools, jerked Lanson's attention towards Burges. The physicist blew on his fingers with pain, and glared reproachfully at them.

'What's the matter, Burges? Want any help?'

'About time you asked me that, Lanson.' Burges frowned, and examined his fingers. He was a small, wrinkled man, with a mop of thin, white hair and a perpetually worried expression. A dirty laboratory smock covered his untidy uniform, and his eyes were vague behind thick lensed spectacles.

'Come and hold this while I solder the connections. If I burn my fingers once more, they won't be of any use at all.'

Lanson laughed and moved across to the bench. He looked with interest at the maze of tangled wires half soldered to a frame of complex angles and various metals. Bender joined him silently.

Together they held the slender wires while the old physicist rapidly soldered them to glistening connections. He hummed to himself as he worked, utterly oblivious to the quivering of the walls and the chatter of the geigers. Bender looked down at the mop of white hair.

'What made you join the insurgents, Burges?'

The physicist shrugged. 'They tried to stop my research, said that it was illogical to pursue pure science.' He snorted, and reached for more flex. 'They wanted me to concentrate on food production, abandon the work of a lifetime; of course I couldn't allow that.'

'So you came here with us and loaded our torpedoes with atomic explosives bred from the pile.' Lanson glanced at the squat bulk of the small atomic pile, which together with its mercury boilers, humped in one corner. 'What are you doing now?'

'Trying to finish my work.'

'Finish your work!' Bender snorted with disgust. 'Don't you realise that we'll all be dead within a few hours? What's the use of finishing something you'll never be able to use anyway? Why waste your time like this?'

'Bender!' Lanson stared warningly at the younger man. He smiled at the old physicist. 'What is it that you are trying to do?'

'Whatever it is I'm not sitting down twiddling my thumbs, like some people I know.' Burges glared at the blond young man. 'He talks like a logician, like one of those cold-blooded fools who wanted me to give up my work. If everyone thought like that, if they stopped to value what they did before they did it, nothing would ever get done.' He turned to fuss with his work.

'He's a bit high strung,' soothed Lanson. 'We all are. After all we haven't anything to occupy our minds as you have.'

'Is that my fault?' Burges snorted, then calmed himself as he began to fit the frame with its tangle of wires to a partly assembled machine. Lanson stared at it with interest. It seemed to be made of hastily fashioned metal and plastic. Crude, unfinished, and yet built with a rugged strength and natural skill. A mass of coils and tubes wreathed a large circular opening. He stared through it, and he saw the humped bulk of the atomic pile beyond. A control board, studded with dials and switches, was joined to both the strange machine and to the power output board of the atomic pile.

'What is it?'

'The product of a lifetime,' said Burges. 'Pure mathematics in a concrete form. I evolved the mathematical concepts over a period of years, testing equations, discarding them for new and better ones. The electronic brain at the university

13

helped me, without it the calculations would have taken more years than there are in a normal lifetime. Now it is almost finished.'

'Almost?'

'An hour or two at the most. It takes time for the power to accumulate.'

'I see.' Lanson frowned in thought. 'This means a lot to you, doesn't it?'

'It has been my life's work,' Burges said simply. He caressed the machine with one thin hand. 'To prove my equations are correct, to open a path to other worlds — ' His voice died in silence.

'Maybe I can get you that extra time.' Lanson spun to face Bender. 'Get me contact on the radio to the attacking force. Hurry!'

'What are you going to do, Lanson?' Hope flared in the young man's eyes. 'Is there a way out?'

'Perhaps, but at least we needn't die like vermin. I'm going to ask for time.' He smiled at the old scientist. 'At least you'll see if your machine does work or not.'

'It will.' The old man seemed very certain. 'It is merely a question of providing time, for the power to accumulate.'

'We shall see.' Lanson turned to where Bender crouched over a humming radio. 'Have you made contact yet?'

The radio spluttered, squealing with static and the crackling sound of broken atoms. It steadied, and a man's voice, cold, emotionless, strangely non-human, echoed through the chamber.

'Yes?'

'Lanson speaking. Lanson of the Free Army.'

'Yes?'

'I and two others are in the strongpoint under attack. I ask for terms.'

'Why?'

'Isn't that obvious?' Lanson tried to keep the sneer out of his voice. 'We wish to live.'

'Will you accept treatment?'

'Yes,' lied the tall commander. He looked at the others. 'We all agree to accept De Bracy's drug.' Silence while the radio hummed and tension slowly mounted.

'It would be easier to blast you all to dust,' mused the cold, hard voice.

'Easier, but illogical,' snapped Lanson. 'Why kill when there is no need to destroy? There is valuable equipment here, an atomic pile, other things. We are ready to surrender, you have no good reason for killing us and destroying the strongpoint.'

'How will you emerge? The escape tunnels have been demolished.'

'We must wait until the surface radioactivity has died. There is a second escape tunnel but we cannot use it for several hours.' Sweat glistened on Lanson's features as he stared at the softly humming radio.

'I will give you two hours, at the end of that time the strongpoint will be demolished with H-type bombs.' The cold voice had not altered its tone as it pronounced sentence. The radio died as the current ceased to flow.

Lanson grinned triumphantly at Burges.

2

Worlds of if

Bender sat on one corner of the cluttered workbench and stared at the dully glinting machine squatting in the centre of the chamber. His mouth twitched, and from time to time he passed a hand through his hair. Lanson, busy helping Burges with parts of the strange machine, grinned at him.

'What's the matter, Bender?'

'Nothing.'

Lanson crossed the chamber and sat down beside him. 'I know how it is,' he said quietly. 'We all of us want to live, but how can we? Two hours isn't enough to emerge from here, even if we could. The surface radioactivity wouldn't have died by then, and we'd all be burnt.'

'Isn't there something we could do?' Bender clenched his hands, the knuckles gleaming white in the dull blue glow. 'I'm as ready to die as the next man, but just to sit here and wait!'

'Come and help Burges,' suggested Lanson. 'Talk to him, it will help keep your mind off what's coming.'

'H-type bombs,' muttered Bender. 'We could stand one, maybe two, but never three. Nothing ever built could. How they must hate us!'

'Let's talk to Burges.' Lanson slid from the end of the bench and dragged the reluctant Bender with him. The old physicist stepped back from his machine as they approached and grinned.

'All finished. I'll begin to feed in the power now, and the rest is just a matter of time.'

'What is it?' Bender sounded utterly disinterested as he stared at the crude machine.

'I told you, a machine with which I hope to be able to see other worlds.' Burges stepped to the control board and slowly swung rheostats. Needles flickered, a faint whine came from the mercury boilers, and a row of little red lamps flashed, then died. Burges stepped back.

'Nothing to do now but wait. It will take a lot of power, but I have the entire output of an atomic pile to draw on.'

'Other worlds?' Lanson looked at the old man with a faint gleam of hope shining in his deep black eyes. 'Mars? Venus? Where?'

'Not other planets,' snapped Burges. 'Other worlds.' He smiled apologetically. 'I'm sorry. I've lived with this thing for so long that I can't remember that others don't know as much about it as I do.' He seated himself on the workbench. 'Have you heard of the theory of alternate universes? Simultaneous worlds?'

'No.' Lanson looked at Bender. 'Have you?'

'No.'

'I think that you'd better explain,' Lanson said ruefully. 'We both seem to be pretty ignorant.'

Burges sighed and settled himself more comfortably on the edge of the bench.

'You know, of course, that life is made up of moments of decision. There are times when each individual has a choice, he can either do one thing, or we can do another. For example, you could take De Bracy's treatment, but you chose not to. You could have surrendered when first asked, or you could have decided to fight. You understand me?'

'I think so.' Lanson slowly nodded. 'If I had chosen differently, then I wouldn't be here now. I could have taken the treatment, I could have surrendered, but I didn't, and now I have no choice left to me.'

'Exactly. Now suppose that you had taken the treatment, you would then have lived in a world that is a little different to this one, a world in which you would not have fought, men would not have died, and where you would have been respected instead of being hunted down to your death.'

'Yes, but all that is in the past.'

'Yes, in our past I agree, but it is possible that a world in which you chose differently does exist. We are not aware of it, of course, but theoretically it could exist.' Burges paused and smiled at his machine. 'I have proved that it does exist.'

'What!' Bender leaned forward eagerly.

'Let me get this straight. You mean that there is more than one universe existing at the same time?'

'I mean that there is an infinity of universes all existing at the same time.' Burges said calmly. 'My equations prove it, and this machine will prove my equations to be correct.'

Lanson wiped sweat from his face and neck and fumbled for a cigarette. The air fans had stopped and the heat was growing oppressive. Faint murmurs came from the machine, and needles quivered on the dial-covered control board.

'I think that I begin to understand,' he said quietly. 'If Wilner had not reached the Moon in his revolutionary atomic space ship. If De Bracy had not perfected his drug. If Conroy had not discovered controllable atomic fission, then the world would not be as we know it.' He frowned through a haze of blue smoke. 'It must be something like a fan.'

Burges nodded and rested his hand down on the bench, the fingers out-stretched and splayed.

'Imagine the palm to be a point of

decision,' he ordered. 'We can take De Bracy's drug as an example. Now what could have happened? The drug works, that is the palm. People could have refused to take it; that is the first finger. They could have taken it, but not made its use compulsory; that is the second finger. The government could have outlawed its use; that is the third finger. The Free Army could have won its battle with the Logicians; that is the little finger. Or the Logicians could have won the war with the Free Army; that is the thumb, and that is what happened. Five worlds from one point of decision.'

'They would become more and more unlike as time passed,' murmured Lanson.

'Yes, and of course, from the main branches there would be other minor ones. An infinity of worlds, all differing from each other in minor detail, some differing so much as to be unrecognizable, but all very close.'

'That means that somewhere there is a world in which we three are sitting just as we are now, but we have brown uniforms instead of black.' Bender shook his head.

'It sounds incredible.'

'It is true!' Burges stepped across to the control board and slowly adjusted a rheostat. 'I shall prove it.'

'How?'

'With this.' He gestured towards the machine with its enigmatic circle. Lanson looked at it again; aside from the fact that it seemed to be absorbing a titanic amount of power, it seemed just as before. He squinted through the circle, the humped bulk of the atomic pile wavered a little as he watched.

'What does it do?'

'The machine? Nothing.' Burges grinned at Lanson's blank expression. 'It doesn't fly, doesn't throw a ray or a beam, it is merely an accumulator.'

'It's certainly drinking power.' Lanson looked at the dials and pursed his lips in a soundless whistle. 'Where's it all going?'

Burges chuckled. 'Nowhere. It's still in the machine.' He settled himself again on the edge of the bench. 'The machine is based on a well-known scientific fact. If you take a coil of lead wire, and immerse that coil in liquid helium, you utterly

23

destroy its resistance to an electric current. An electrical impulse will run round and round the coil without loss of energy. Naturally this only applies while it is immersed.'

'I know that cold decreases the resistance of a conductor,' agreed Lanson. 'What has this to do with alternate worlds?'

'Everything. I reasoned that if a coil so chilled would contain an electrical current without loss, then a larger coil, chilled to almost absolute zero, would have interesting phenomena. It did.'

'I took a coil of chemically pure lead, treated it with a cyclotron to alter its atomic balance, immersed it in liquid helium, and fed in power. I fed in a lot of power, so much that the field currents within the coil distorted normal space. The strains of the trapped electricity were too great for normal space to contain, so they made their own space.'

'Then what?'

'For a moment I looked at another world.' Burges sighed and shrugged. 'That was just before the Logicians came for me. I haven't had a chance to repeat the experiment until now.'

'I see.' Lanson began to stride impatiently about the chamber. 'You say that you could see another world. What was it like?'

'Very much the same as ours. Why?'

'Could it have been ours?'

'No. I put my hand behind the coil, but I couldn't see it. Why do you ask?'

'If you could see another world, is there any reason why you could not have gone through the coil and entered it?' Lanson was breathing rather fast. Burges frowned.

'I've never thought about it, I suppose it could be done. Why?'

'Why?' Lanson grinned at Bender and shook his head. 'Don't you understand that you have had the means for us to escape certain death, and haven't said anything about it? If your machine works, and you seem confident that it will, what's to prevent us going through the circle?'

'Why nothing.' The old physicist stared in sudden understanding. 'Of course! We can leave here, enter an alternate world one in which the Logicians do not exist.'

He bent his head in sudden emotion. 'I was so certain that I was going to die,' he muttered. 'Now I can carry on with my work.'

Lanson glanced at the watch strapped to his wrist. 'We'd better hurry,' he snapped. 'Our time limit is almost over. Can't you speed things up a little?'

'I don't want to feed power in too fast,' explained Burges, adjusting the controls. 'There is no danger of heating the coil. I'm using both chemical and electrical methods of cooling, but the pressure is mounting fast.'

'Can you adjust the direction,' Bender asked. 'Remember we are five hundred feet below the ground, we don't want to be buried alive.'

'I have some degree of control, a little. But enough to ensure that we arrive on the surface.'

'Can you pick where we're going to land?' Lanson tugged at the lobe of his ear. 'I'd like to get as far from the Logicians and their devilish drug as possible.'

'The amount of power in the coil

determines that. The warp will open out on an alternate world, but which one I have no method of telling. We must take our chances.'

'Good enough.' Lanson glanced at Bender. 'Better get a few things together, we don't know what might come in useful. Weapons, of course, two flare guns each and as many spare charges as we can carry. A medical kit, and what small instruments we can take without unnecessary bother.' He glanced at his watch. 'Better hurry.'

For a while they bustled about the crowded chamber collecting what they could conveniently carry. Burges hovered over the control panel, coaxing extra power from the labouring dynamos. He glanced worriedly at Lanson.

'How much time do we have? I'm afraid of the coil, there is so much power trapped within it, that the slightest jar might cause it to burst. If it does, the result will make an atomic bomb look like a candle by comparison.'

'Can't we ask for extra time?' Bender glanced at the radio.

'Try them,' snapped Lanson. He peered through the circle. It seemed to be filled with coiling mist. The humped bulk of the atomic pile and the smooth curve of the mercury boiler was gone, the mist swirled, twisted upon itself. He stepped back rubbing at his eyes.

'The warp is building,' muttered Burges. 'A little more power and it will break through, we shall have to move fast when it does.'

Bender crouched over the radio, his face white and his fingers trembling as he turned the dials. The set hummed, crackled, settled to a smooth purr. A man's voice snapped cold questions.

'Yes?'

Bender gestured to Lanson, stepped aside from the set.

'Lanson here. Commander of the Free Army. We are almost free of the strong-point, will you extend the time limit?'

'No.'

'I ask for a few extra minutes, ten or fifteen. We are almost free and can make it in that time. Will you grant us an extension?'

'No.'

'You are being illogical,' Lanson snapped.

'I am dropping H-type bombs in exactly seven minutes.' The radio clicked and was silent.

'If I didn't know differently I swear that he has a sense of humour,' Lanson said grimly. 'You heard him, Burges. We have exactly seven minutes, nearer six now. Can you speed things up?'

'I'm trying,' gasped the old man. The whine of the dynamos grew louder, echoing through the small chamber with a song of sheer power. The heat increased, sweat ran down their eyes stinging with salt. Impatiently Bender tore at his tunic.

'Keep it on,' snapped Lanson. 'You'll need it where we're going.' He glanced at his wrist. 'Three minutes.'

A cry came from the old physicist. He pointed at the circle with a quivering finger. 'Look! We're through!'

The mist had cleared. A gentle slope of vivid green showed beyond the circle, a rolling lawn covered with lush grass and framed by a blue sky. The thin spires of a city showed dimly on the far horizon, and something that looked like a bird, but could have been a machine, soared against the blue of the sky.

'Let's go,' snapped Lanson. He moved towards the old physicist. 'You first.'

'Be careful of the edge,' warned the old man. 'Don't touch it, if you do you will release the stored energy.' He looked helplessly around. 'How shall we get through?'

'Like this!' Lanson nodded to Bender. 'Ready?'

Together they picked up the small man, swung him, swung him again.

'One,' gasped Lanson. 'Two! Three!' The small physicist spun through the air. He twisted, almost touched the edge of the coil, then rolled on the green grass beyond the circle.

'Now you,' snapped Lanson. He glanced at his watch and stared at the low roof. 'Hurry!'

Bender nodded, took a short run, and flung himself at the circle. Lanson threw the equipment after him, the flare guns, the spare charges, the medical kit and other things that they had gathered. He tensed himself, started to run, and was suddenly flung against the side of the chamber.

Dust filled the air. The machine quivered in sympathy with the walls, and for a moment the rolling slope in the circle flickered, blanked out, then returned. Before the second bomb could fall Lanson had flung himself through the air towards safety.

Something gripped him, seemed to twist his stomach and stop his breath, then he was through, rolling on the soft, green grass.

'Get away!' he yelled. 'Keep clear — the bombs — '

A gout of emerald green force exploded beside him. It lashed at the ground, charring the grass and incinerating the soil. For a moment it stabbed, an almost solid beam of pure force, then it died, and the smell of ozone hung heavily on the air.

Lanson climbed shakily to his feet. Bender joined him. Burges lay silent on the ground.

'Burges! Are you all right?' Lanson bent

over the small figure and turned him over.

Burges gasped, then struggled to his feet. 'You winded me, throwing me like that,' he complained. His eyes widened as he saw the scorched ground. 'It went?'

'Yes. The bombs set it off.' Lanson picked up the few articles lying around. The flare guns were intact, so was most of the ammunition, and the medical kit. The rest had been destroyed.

He stood for a while taking deep breaths of the cool air, then narrowed his eyes at something he saw in the distance.

'Hide your guns,' he said quietly. 'We've got company.'

Together they waited on the brow of the slope.

3

The Star People

A vehicle moved slowly across the green sward towards them, a low-slung car, with hidden wheels and tapering body. It was coloured a brilliant red and green with transparent windows, and a low turret supported the slender barrel of what appeared to be a weapon. It hissed softly as it moved, little wisps of steam hovering in the still air behind it.

'It must have come from the city,' Lanson murmured. 'Someone saw the flash as the coil spilled its energy, and have come to investigate.'

'They came fast then,' Bender whispered. 'We only got through a few minutes ago.' He licked his dry lips. 'Shall we run?'

'No. We're here, and it's up to us to make the best of it. We've got to establish contact sooner or later, and it may as well be now.' Lanson glanced at the physicist. 'What do you make of that vehicle, Burges?'

'Steam driven, armed, probably very fast and certainly very powerful.' The old man shrugged. 'War or police vehicle.'

'Why powerful?' Bender stared at the nearing vehicle. 'It looks clumsy to me, and it's moving slowly enough.'

'Look at the size of it, almost forty feet long and about ten high, that takes power to move.' The old man grinned at Bender. 'Don't ever get the wrong impression about steam power, it's one of the most powerful forces we know.' He fell silent as the machine hissed to a halt a few feet from the foot of the slope.

A door slid open, and three men leapt lightly onto the grass. They were dressed in a trim uniform of red and green, with high knee boots of polished black. Two of the men held weapons cradled in their arms, the third a pistol in his hand. Golden insignia glittered on his left breast and shoulder.

The two men deployed smartly to

either side, their cradled weapons menacing the little group on the brow of the slope. The officer halted several feet from them, well out of the line of fire. He glanced at the seared grass, then at the three waiting men, his eyes widening as he saw their black and gold uniforms.

'How came you here?' His accent was slight, and the language familiar. Lanson breathed a sigh of relief.

'We are from a far place,' he said carefully. 'Strangers to your land, but friends of your people. Where are we?'

'It is the forbidden zone of the city of Zytlen, home of the Star People.'

'The Star People?'

'Yes.' The officer stared at them with narrowed eyes. 'The penalty of unauthorised entry is death.'

He levelled the clumsy looking pistol in his hand, and the two watching men aimed their cradled weapons. The turret of the huge land car swung a little, the slender nozzle pointing at the little group.

'Before you die,' said the officer casually, 'I must ask for your names and occupations, place of birth and place of employment.'

'My name is Lanson. I am a space pilot.'

'I am Bender. An astrogator.'

'Burges, a physicist.'

The officer blinked, and lowered his pistol.

'A space pilot?'

'Yes.'

'You mean that you have piloted ships through space?'

'Yes.'

'I see.' The officer hesitated, then looked at Bender. 'What is an astrogator?'

'A man who is able to plot a course through the heavens, to guide a space ship so that it will arrive at its destination.'

'And a physicist?'

'A student of natural science,' said Burges dryly.

The officer drew a deep breath, and glanced towards the watching guards. 'Put up your weapons.' He gestured to the softly hissing land car. 'I must ask you to enter.'

'The alternative?' Lanson smiled tightly, his hand beneath his tunic gripping the butt of a flare gun.

'You have no choice,' The officer pointed towards the nozzle protruding from the turret. 'Enter or die!'

He stood politely aside as they clambered within the strange vehicle.

It was hot inside, and the thick air was tainted with the fumes of oil. The skin was of metal, as were the floorplates and bulkheads. A narrow passage led from the entrance port to the control room where a man sat on a high seat his hands resting on a bank of levers. Other passages led to various parts of the vehicle. Lanson glanced down them as they were ushered into the control room, but the turret seemed to be sealed, and he caught only a glimpse of the engine room.

Metal clanged, and the officer snapped curt orders. The man on the high seat shifted a lever, steam hissed, and with a slight jerk the car began to move forward. It picked up speed with a smooth surge of power, and Burges grinned at the startled expression on Bender's face.

'I told you that steam was powerful,' he chuckled. He glanced at the officer who stood staring out of the transparent windows, then leaned across to Lanson.

'Did you notice their weapons?' he whispered. 'Thick barrelled, clumsy-looking things, they remind me of the old muzzle loading, black powder guns.'

'I noticed,' Lanson said softly. 'Keep your flare guns out of sight, I don't think the officer knows that we are armed and he can't be used to such compact weapons.'

The officer turned and stared curiously at them. He snapped orders to the man at the controls, then crossed the small room and stood beside them.

'You are strange men,' he said abruptly. 'You are wearing a uniform which I have never seen before. From which city do you come?'

'A far city,' Lanson said cautiously.

The officer nodded as if the answer made sense. 'It may well be,' he murmured. 'I have little knowledge of far places, but the Zytlen will know.'

'The Zytlen?'

'The Star People, the Rulers, the Conquerors of Earth.' His face seemed strangely bitter as he spoke.

'Earth then has been conquered?' Lanson leaned forwards, his eyes intent on the officer's face. It was a young face, yet one made strangely old by a cynical bitterness and an acceptance of fate. He flushed beneath Lanson's calm gaze.

'Have you been sleeping for the past thirty years?' He glanced towards the man at the controls, then lowered his voice. 'Tell me, are you of the Free People?'

'I have fought for freedom,' Lanson answered vaguely. 'Why do you ask?'

'Your friends, are they to be trusted?'

'Yes.'

'I see.' The officer swallowed, then lowered his voice still more. 'Listen, what I tell you could mean my death, and yet there is something about you to be trusted. Is it true that you have knowledge of spatial flight?'

'It is.'

'Good. My name is Serg Val Marco, officer of the Eastern Marches of the city of Zytlen. I am taking you to the city of the Star People for questioning, and I have little doubt that you will never emerge alive. If I enable you to escape, what would be your plans?'

Lanson shrugged. 'We have none, we are strangers in a strange place. We need friends to hide us, books and tapes from which to learn, a thousand things. You must help us.'

'I cannot!' Sweat glistened on Marco's face. 'I tell you that it would mean my life if you were to repeat what I have told you. I am willing to help you to escape, more I cannot do.'

'Where could we go if we escaped?'

'There are woods to the north, thick woods which prevent entry of ground cars. Rumour has it that the Free People have a camp there.'

'I see, and which direction is north?'

'We are heading there now. Well?' Lanson grinned, and suddenly swung his clenched fist.

Marco grunted and slumped unconscious in Lanson's arms. Quickly he lowered the young officer to the metal flooring, and jerked his head at his two companions, gesturing towards the open passageways. Silently he strode across the control room towards the man sitting in the high chair.

Something must have warned him, he turned, stared at Lanson then at the slumped figure of his officer. He reached frantically for a lever, his mouth opening to yell a warning.

Lanson caught him around the throat, applied quick and expert pressure to vital nerves, and let the unconscious man slump to the floor. 'Bender,' he snapped. 'Get the rest of the crew. Don't kill them unless you have to, but be careful.' He stared at the complex levers before him. 'Burges, can you operate this machine?'

'I can try.' The old physicist slipped into the driving seat and began testing the controls. The car lurched beneath them, swung a little, then moved forward at increased speed. 'Which way?'

'North. There should be an instrument something like a compass; if you can't find it, steer by the sun, or by the stars, or by guesswork, but keep heading north.'

Lanson ran down a passageway from which came sounds of combat.

Bender crouched behind an angle, his flare gun in his hand, an ugly wound across his forehead. He grinned as Lanson joined him, and gestured with the flare gun.

'There's three of them around there. They almost got me with one of their fancy weapons, but I ducked in time. Shall I burn them out?'

'No.' Lanson peered round the angle, then jerked his head back to safety. Something boomed and metal rang as a bullet smashed against the wall. He kicked at a flattened button of lead.

'Muzzle loaders, the old man was right.' He raised his voice and shouted above the hiss of the engine. 'You there, come out with your hands empty or I'll roast you alive.'

Someone laughed and began to call out, his words lost in the deep roar of a weapon. The bullet smacked against the opposite wall, ricocheted with a thin whine, and plucked at Lanson's sleeve. He glanced down with a twisted smile.

'They're learning, that was an iron bullet.' He drew a flare gun, spun the focussing control to wide aperture, and fired a charge upwards against the metal of the roof.

Searing energy filled the narrow passageway. Heat lashed from the metal walls and roof, raising the temperature of the air almost to boiling point. Silence followed the roar of the discharge.

'The next one will be aimed low,' called Lanson. 'Coming out now?'

Weapons clattered on the floorplates, and three men staggered around the angle of the passage. They moaned as they walked, their hands clasped over their singed flesh, but the expression in their eyes was one of horror.

'The Star People!' One of the men babbled the words. 'The weapons of the Overlords. Mercy, sir. Mercy!'

'Silence! How many are in your crew?'

'Five, sir. Just five.'

'Good.' Lanson turned to Bender. 'Tell Burges to stop the ground car, these people can walk back.' He gestured with the flare gun. 'Quick now. Move!'

It was soon done. The huge vehicle shuddered to a halt, the three slightly burned men, and the two unconscious ones were gathered on the grass outside. The doors clanged shut, and the car moved effortlessly on its way. Lanson bit his lip with thought as he stared at the dwindling figures of the crew.

'He was lying,' he snapped. 'There must be more than five crew. Bender, help me search the car.'

'Why should there be more than five?' protested the young man. 'One driver, one in the turret, and three who came outside. Five. It makes sense to me.'

'Not to me,' snapped Lanson. 'This vehicle is too big for just five men. Quick now, help me to search.'

They found the man in the engine room.

He was twisted, almost blind, burnt and scarred with unshielded radiation. He cowered in a corner, cables trailing from clips fastened to his wrists, and he mewed to himself from a tongueless mouth. The place stank of heat and oil and the odour of unwashed flesh. Lanson shuddered.

'Get back,' he snapped to Bender. 'This place is rotten with radiation.' He squinted at the humped bulk of the engine, noticed that the trailing cables led to a connection in one wall, and stared at the fluorescent lighting.

'The swine,' he muttered. 'The filthy, inhuman swine.'

'What is it?' asked Bender.

'Their method of control, don't you understand? This car is powered with an atomic engine, they use fissionable material, probably U235 to generate intense heat. That, that *thing* in there is their method of control.'

'How?'

'You noticed the electrical cables attached to his arms, didn't you? They probably send impulses through them, and he either retracts or advances the rods as required. They would have a safety stop, of course, but his job is to bring two or more masses of fissionable material nearer to each other, or further apart whichever is needed. The nearer they are, the more heat generated, and thus the more steam, when they wish to lower steam pressure, he draws them apart.'

'I can't see it. Why not use remote control?'

'How do I know?' snarled Lanson. 'Perhaps they find it cheaper to use men. The whole engine room is contaminated with radioactivity, it must leak throughout the entire vehicle. That man in there is almost blind, they've cut out his tongue to stop his screams, and they stab him with electricity to make him jump and obey orders.'

He stared at his clenched hands, the knuckles white with strain. 'Somehow,' he said very quietly, 'somehow I don't think I'm going to like the Zytlen one little bit.'

Bender followed him silently towards the control room.

For hours they moved across the rolling green countryside. The sun swung in the clear blue sky, and stars began to twinkle high in the heavens. The ground car slid easily at a fairly high speed, and Lanson tried to forget the poor wretch chained in the engine room. Towards night, when the black shadows were pressing against the edges of the dying day, something loomed on the far horizon.

Burges pointed, shifted uncomfortably on his hard metal seat.

'Those must be the woods, Lanson.'

'Good. We'll get as near as we can, and then leave the car. I'll be glad to get out of this radioactive death trap. I wonder if Marco knew what was happening to him.'

Bender shrugged. 'He seemed contented enough.'

'He would do, until his hair began falling out, his skin breaking into running sores, his bones softening, and his blood becoming devoid of white corpuscles. He wouldn't guess that he was becoming sterile, not unless he was married that is, and he'd probably die before he went blind.'

Bender shuddered. 'Is it as bad as that?' he whispered.

'Yes. If we had a geiger counter here, it would rattle itself apart. That engine room was designed by someone with a total disregard for human life. The Star People,' Lanson said bitterly, 'must find humans very cheap.'

The woods grew nearer, a grim tangle of trees and undergrowth, black and vaguely menacing in the dim starlight.

The car shuddered to a halt, and Burges clambered gratefully off the metal seat.

'This is as near as we can get,' he announced. 'We'll have to walk the rest.'

'Suits me,' agreed Bender. 'The sooner I'm out of here the better I'll like it.' He looked at Lanson. 'How about that man in the engine room?'

'We'll try and find help, then come back for him.' Lanson checked his flare guns, and slipped them into the holsters beneath his tunic. 'Ready?'

Together they jumped from the warm, oily atmosphere of the softly hissing ground car. The clean smell of growing things blew gently from the woods, and gratefully Lanson drew a deep breath.

'Gently now,' he warned. 'If there are any people here we don't want them to shoot us.'

He took three steps forward, then flung himself down as something flashed past his head.

4

Earth enslaved

It came from behind him, from the direction of the ground car, and desperately he twisted in the clinging undergrowth as the strange weapon flashed again. Fire blossomed to one side, sudden searing flame shriveling the undergrowth, and stinging unprotected flesh with fierce heat.

'The turret!' Bender thrashed on the ground beating at his smoldering tunic. 'Someone is firing from the turret!'

Dimly against the star-studded sky, Lanson could see the slender nozzle of the turret gun waver as it sought its aim. Something crashed in the woods, an animal leaping for shelter, and the nozzle steadied, spat a thin jet of fire. A bush exploded into lambent flame, and for a few seconds the dying animal screamed with pain.

Lanson rolled, steadying his elbow on

the soft loam. The flare gun in his hand roared its note of destruction, and searing energy blazed from the pitted muzzle. The blast caught against the turret, turning the metal to cherry red. He fired again, then again, the third shot searing clean through the slender nozzle.

Abruptly the turret spouted into flame.

'Back!' yelled Lanson. 'Get back! The whole thing's going to explode!'

Desperately they plunged through the tangled mass of undergrowth, crashing into trees, and tripping over hidden roots. Behind them a column of flame rose to the sky, hissing and flaring with tremendous energy, turning night into day.

Lanson flung himself down behind a fallen tree, grabbing at Bender and the old physicist as they stumbled past.

'Get down,' he ordered, gasping for breath. 'It's going up any moment now.'

Tensely they waited, shielding their eyes from the burning brilliance of the turret, trying to still the mad pounding of their hearts, and cringing against the soft loam of the forest floor.

Something shook them. It filled the

night with flame and noise, soaring high into the darkness and hissing back to earth. Sound tore at their ears, cruel light stabbed at their tightly shut eyes, and their skins crawled to the impact of radiation. Then it was over, and aside from a few small fires, the night was still.

Of the huge ground car, there was no trace except a smoking hole in the soft loam and a few scattered fragments of twisted metal.

Lanson sighed, and turned so that his head rested against the bulk of the fallen tree. He lay there, staring at the spangled stars, and feeling fatigue seep through his overstrained body, remembered that he had not slept for more than four days. Suddenly he felt very tired.

Burges had curled into a ball, his head with its mop of white hair cradled against an arm.

Bender stirred restlessly, looking at the spot where the ground car had rested. 'I could have sworn that thing was empty.'

'It was,' murmured Lanson tiredly. 'That turret was robot controlled. The Zytlen whoever they are, obviously don't trust men too much. They kept radio control of the turret, probably had it linked to television screens so that they could see everything that was happening. When we had led them as far as we intended, the operator tried to kill us. Luckily for us it was dark and he had to rely on the sonar equipment, otherwise we wouldn't have been here now. When I'd disabled the turret, he blew up the car to prevent it falling into our hands. Clever.'

Bender mumbled something, then sighed and slumped into sleep. Lanson grinned, slipped one of his flare guns from its holster, and tucked it beneath the tree, the other he held in his hand. He fumbled for cigarettes, then remembered he shouldn't smoke while on watch.

He fell asleep trying to decide why.

Something touched his eyes, his nose, his face. For a moment he lay quietly letting memory flood back to his tired brain, and wondering what it was that touched him so gently. Slowly he opened his eyes, then closed them again and rolled to one side. It was daylight that had touched him, and he had stared straight into the sun.

He sat up, looking a little stupidly at the flare gun still clutched in one hand, then he remembered and recovered the other one from beneath the tree. He stretched, yawned, and rubbed his eyes. He became conscious of raging hunger. He grinned down at the softly snoring figures of his two companions, and shook them awake. They sighed luxuriously, enjoying to the full the release from continuous mental and physical pain.

'I'm hungry,' complained Bender. He ruffled his thick, blond curls, and grinned at Lanson. 'When do they serve breakfast?'

'When we get it.' Lanson rose to his feet, and stretched again. He glanced round at the tangled undergrowth, his eyes suddenly narrowing with understanding. Slowly he sat down.

From the denseness of a thicket, a small round circle stared at them. Another peered behind the trunk of a tree, a third from above a clump of grass. As he let his eyes drift around him, he spotted still more of the little circles. They were surrounded by the muzzles of pointing guns.

Bender stared at him in puzzled wonder. 'What's the matter, Lanson? You look as if you'd seen a ghost.'

'We've got company,' he said quietly. 'No, don't — ' He halted Bender's instinctive motion towards his flare guns. 'They've got us covered from all angles, one false move and we'll be riddled like a sieve.'

'Where are they?' Burges peered at the undergrowth. 'I can't see a thing.'

Lanson smiled, and shook his head at the old man's bewilderment. 'All right,' he called. 'We're awake now, and we know that you're covering us. What do you want?'

The bushes rustled, and a man stepped into the clearing.

He was a big man, tall and broad in proportion. He had short, cropped hair, and one side of his face was twisted with glistening scar tissue. He stood easily on the balls of his feet, a pistol in one hand, and stared at them from his one good eye.

'My name is Ben Ley Marvin,' he said. 'Who are you?'

'That's Burges,' Lanson pointed towards the old physicist. 'I'm Lanson, and this is Bender.'

'Short names,' said the big man suspiciously.

'It is the custom where we come from to only have one name,' explained Lanson tiredly.

'Where would that be?'

'A far place.' Lanson clutched at the tree for support. His head swam and he felt a burning sickness at the pit of his stomach. 'Please, if you have any food, we'd be grateful.'

'Are you ill?'

'Yes, a little radiation sickness, we got it when the ground car exploded last night. Rest and food will put us right.'

'I see.' Marvin gestured towards the bushes. 'Can you walk? It isn't far, but remember, you'll be covered every inch of the way.'

'We can walk,' promised Lanson, 'and we won't forget.'

Together they threaded their way

deeper into the woods.

The encampment was cunningly hidden, camouflaged by trees and undergrowth so that it was impossible to see from the air, and hardly noticeable from the ground. Small fires burned in stone fireplaces, and a knot of men looked up as they approached.

Like Marvin they were dressed in old remnants of uniforms, faded and patched so that the original color was lost, and identification impossible. Some wore skin caps, others leather, and all carried a long-barrelled weapon, which together with a knife, seemed to be general equipment.

Food was brought to them in wooden bowls, and the three companions gratefully swallowed hot stew, and chewed on lumps of hard, black bread. Marvin sat silent while they ate, the scar tissue on his face giving him a sinister appearance, his one eye taking in every detail of their uniforms and general accoutrements.

Lanson finished the food, and fumbled for his cigarette. The simple act of smoking seemed to startle the watching men, and Marvin laughed.

'One thing's certain,' he said in his deep voice. 'You're not from any city, the serfs of the Zytlen do not smoke.'

'Do you?' Lanson held out the packet, Marvin shook his head.

'We used to, but the tobacco ran out and leaves are a poor substitute.' He stared curiously at the three men. 'Care to tell me about it now?'

'Yes.' Lanson looked at Burges, then shrugged. 'I'll tell it. We have come from an alternative world to this. I don't know if you can understand what I mean, but it seems that there are an infinity of universes all existing at the same time. We are from one where the Zytlen as you call them are unknown.'

'Simultaneous worlds.' Marvin nodded. 'I have read of the theory.'

'You know of that theory?' Burges leaned forward excitedly. 'From what the officer who captured us said, I thought that all research and knowledge had died.'

'No.' Marvin settled himself more comfortably in the bracken. 'We are not as ignorant as we seem. Up to thirty years ago we had a very high technology, then the Zytlen came, and our civilization crumpled.'

'I'd like to find out just when the split from our own universe occurred.' Burges hunched forward on his knees.

'Did Wilner reach the Moon?'

'Wilner?' Marvin frowned, then his face cleared. 'Yes, it was just after that when the ship of the Zytlen landed.'

'I see, then, of course, Conroy had discovered the secret of controlled fission?'

'Naturally. Wilner's revolutionary moon rocket was powered with his atomic fuel.'

'How soon did the Zytlen land after Wilner reached the Moon?'

'Not long, about a year. Why?'

'I can tell you why,' Lanson interrupted. 'After the successful flight of Wilner, at least three new-type space ships were ready for flight within a year of that time. If the Zytlen landed when you say they did, then those ships were built and ready for flight. Is that true?'

'I don't know.' Marvin shook his head at Lanson's impatient gesture. 'Remember that when the Star People came, the world was plunged into chaos. The material damage was slight, but the death role was terrific. They orbited the planet with their space ship, and threatened to destroy all life unless we surrendered. When I tell you that the known population of the world is now only one hundred millions, you can see what I mean.'

'How did they do that?' Lanson frowned. 'Even if our losses were heavy, we should have been able to wipe out a mere ship load of the invaders.'

'Agreed, but we never came to close quarters.' Marvin sounded strangely bitter. 'I was alive then, a youth just old enough to carry a gun. They beamed us from their space ship, and men died like flies. We tried, of course. Rocket-planes, guided missiles, we tried them all, but we just couldn't reach them. They were protected by some kind of force field. After every attempt more of our people died, in the end we had to surrender, there was nothing else we could do.'

'I begin to understand.' Lanson nodded as he drew deeply on his cigarette.

'They've settled Earth, split the countries into city states, and turned the people into willing serfs. The feudal system, with the invaders as the rulers, and men and women as their slaves.'

'Yes.'

'Then that car we were captured by, that was a unit of a city's defence force.' Bender snapped his fingers. 'Now I understand why the officer was going to kill us. We were trespassers, outside our territory.'

'Something like that,' agreed Lanson. 'Obviously they patrol their individual areas, and would have investigated the energy release when we came through.' He frowned. 'Marco was going to kill us until he learned that we knew of space flight and natural science. He had no direct contact with the ground car, and so he couldn't have received orders from the robot operator. Why should he save us?'

'The Free People have many sympathisers in the cities,' explained Marvin. 'That young officer was probably one of them. The invasion is still too recent for all pride of race to have been stamped out. Secretly men still hope that the Zytlen may be defeated.'

'Could we use that officer at some later time?'

'No.' Marvin dug the toe of his boot into the soft loam. 'Both he and his crew would have been shot on sight.' He smiled at Bender's startled expression. 'The Zytlen rule with a heavy hand, and they accept no excuses.'

Burges stirred restlessly. He had been examining one of the long-barrelled weapons, and now he looked up with a frown on his wrinkled features.

'If the Zytlen landed only thirty years ago, surely all technological knowledge couldn't have been lost. They couldn't have destroyed all the books and computers, the factories, the men who knew science. Why do you use such poor weapons?'

'What else could we manufacture?' Marvin looked enviously at the flare guns strapped to the old man's waist. 'Remember we have to be very careful, we have nothing but the simplest tools to work with, our power is restricted. We could make better weapons, but we haven't the tools to make them with. We know how to make them, but of what use is that?'

Burges nodded reluctantly. 'Haven't you a research laboratory, trained staff?'

'We have a ruined strongpoint we use as a laboratory. As to trained staff,' Marvin shrugged, 'you can't learn atomics from books. The Zytlen have done everything in their power to destroy all knowledge of atomic science. They have instruments for detecting radiation, and they sterilize any area where they decide excessive radiation may denote the presence of a power pile. One more generation, and atomic science will be a fable of a Golden Age.'

'It all sounds pretty hopeless,' said Bender. He stared into the heart of one of the small fires. 'We could have picked a better world, one in which our training could have been of use. Can we try again?'

'How?' said Burges irritably. 'Where can we obtain an atomic pile for the power we need? The coolant for the coil? All the machine tools and equipment necessary to rebuild the distortion apparatus? It would take a lifetime for one man merely to gather the raw materials. It couldn't be done.'

'It looks as if I'd better learn another trade then,' Bender said ruefully. 'Astrogators don't seem to be of much use in this world.'

'Astrogators?' Marvin wrinkled his brows. 'What's that?'

'I have been trained to plot the course of space ships. Lanson here can pilot them, and that little old man can handle anything appertaining to atomic power.' Bender laughed. 'Our trades are as useful as being able to swim on a world that has no water.'

'I wouldn't say that,' Marvin said softly. He stared at the blue of the heavens just visible between overhanging branches. 'Look up there! Keep looking, you will see something very soon.'

They craned their necks, waiting.

'The Zytlen have always been able to crush us,' the scarred man said quietly. 'They have one weapon we can never overcome. A city tried it once. They revolted, slaughtered the Zytlen, and smashed their equipment. Two hours after they had killed the last of the Star People, the inhabitants of that city lay in a ghastly shambles. They were dead, all of them, men, women and children. They had been killed by a beam from the orbiting space ship.' He pointed upwards. 'There!'

A silver fleck darted across the patch of blue. A gleaming something so bright against the heavens as to be hardly visible. It flashed, twinkled, and was gone.

'There is our enemy,' whispered Marvin. 'Smash that ship, and we can reclaim Earth. While they have it intact, we will die as their slaves.'

Lanson said nothing, but for a long time sat immobile, his eyes fastened on that little patch of blue sky.

5

Into the city

A small fire glowed in the shelter of an overhanging ledge of rock, and a cold wind lashed at the branches of trees. Dim figures huddled about the fire, their features limned by the soft red glow, the low murmur of their conversation almost lost in the sound of the driving wind.

'What are your plans, Lanson?' Marvin leaned forward, the fire glistening strangely on the twisted scar tissue of his face. 'You are well now, your sickness cured. What do you intend?'

'Have we a choice?' Lanson laughed quietly to himself. 'We hoped to find a world at peace, we were tired of war and battle, instead — '

Burges coughed, bracken rustling as he moved his position by the fire. 'What are you getting at, Marvin?'

Bender echoed the question. Like the

others, he too had changed his black and gold uniform for a more serviceable dress of leather and homespun cloth.

'You can help us,' said Marvin. 'Accident, providence, call it what you will, has brought you here.' He paused, looking at them, his one eye gleaming in the red light.

'You are the only men on Earth with the knowledge of space flight. You are the only men on Earth capable of blasting that orbiting space ship from the heavens, of freeing Earth from the invader. Will you do it?'

'How?' asked Lanson curtly.

Marvin shrugged, his broad shoulders slumping as he caught Lanson's meaning. 'I don't know,' he admitted. 'Cooped up here in these woods, in danger of discovery or of instant death if the Zytlen should decide to use their death ray, we can do little. I had hoped that you could help us, perhaps I'd hoped for too much.'

'No,' said Lanson. 'You may hope, but tell me, these woods do not hold all of the Free People, do they?'

'No.'

'I thought as much. You are the very few who are either too well known, or needed for organizational purposes to enter the cities. The race of men cannot have been wholly cowed, not in a mere thirty years. There are others, many of them, alive and free in the cities, waiting for the word to strike. Is that correct?'

Marvin nodded.

'Good.' Lanson smiled, his black eyes like pits in the whiteness of his face. 'We must go to the city.'

'How can we pass undetected?' Bender asked.

'Marvin can help us there. The Free People must have a link with the city dwellers. If they haven't, then they have been wasting their time.'

'We haven't wasted our time.' Marvin poked at the fire, sending red sparks drifting into the damp air. 'We have what you surmise, and more.' He sighed a little. 'I may be making an error, you may not be what you seem, but we must take that chance. Tomorrow I shall give you identification papers, clothes, relevant information and everything you will need to pass undetected. I shall also teach you the various signals we have, passwords, grips, the usual identification methods of any secret organization.' He rose to his feet, big and dark at the edge of the fire.

'If you are not what you claim to be, then you will die horribly.' The very gentleness of his tones added menace to his voice.

Lanson grinned, then shrugged carelessly. 'As you will, Marvin. Burges will stay here with you.'

'Why?' The old physicist lifted his head and glared across the fire.

'You are of far more use here than in the city.' Lanson smiled affectionately at the old man. 'These people need what you can teach them. Remember, you are perhaps the only man alive who understands atomic theory. If we ever do manage to strike a blow at that orbiting space ship, it will be your atomic materials which will make it possible.'

He looked at the black shadow of Marvin. 'How will we communicate with you?'

'All that will be arranged. You will be

contacted in the city, helped as much as possible, but don't rely on us too much.' He hesitated. 'Better leave your weapons with me, they would mean instant death if found on you in the city.'

'No,' protested Bender. 'I wouldn't feel safe without them.'

'We have two weapons each,' decided Lanson. 'We will take one, and a spare magazine of charges, the other and all the rest of the ammunition we will leave with you.'

★   ★   ★

The next day was misty, with a heavy ground fog, and a hint of rain. Marvin peered from the edge of the woods then pointed with one finger. 'Zytlen lies over there. From what you've told me, you must have come further than you needed in that ground car. With luck, you should make the journey within eight hours, but make sure that you miss the patrols.'

'What if we meet them?' asked Bender.

Marvin shrugged. 'You have your weapons,' he said grimly.

Lanson nodded. 'Let's go.'

He strode along with easy strides, breathing deeply of the clean, wet air. Bender managed to keep level with him, glancing at his leader's thin strong face, and trying not to envy his easy carriage.

'Think we'll have trouble?' he blurted after an hour's steady walking.

Lanson shrugged. 'Maybe.'

'What are you going to do in the city?'

'Nothing. We can't do a thing until we know what all this is about. Marvin was plausible, but we only have his word for what has happened.'

'Don't you believe him?' Bender was uncomfortable. 'He convinced me, and after all we did see what was in that ground car.'

'Marvin was telling the truth, as he knew it, but I want to see for myself. The Zytlen may be all he says they are, but I've known men who would do even worse things for the sake of power than these Star People are supposed to have done.'

He laughed at Bender's expression. 'Don't worry about it. We'll look over the city, have a glance at the Zytlen, see what they are and what they seem to be doing. I've my own ideas, and one of them is to take nothing for granted.'

He clutched Bender's arm. 'Can you hear it?'

'What?'

'Listen.'

Softly through the mist came a faint hissing, a metallic clanking and the thud of muffled pistons. Something big and beetle-shaped loomed through the haze.

'A ground car!' Lanson gripped Bender's arm, and flung himself flat on the ground. They were on the rolling smooth green lawn-like area surrounding the city, with not even a bush for cover.

The patrol car came nearer, the slender nozzle in the turret gently swinging from side to side as it approached. Bender grunted, and plunged a hand beneath his short jacket.

'No,' whispered Lanson sharply. 'If we blast this car, they will send air machines, and more cars to comb the entire area. We'd never get out alive.' He watched the lumbering vehicle with narrowed eyes. 'It may miss us. Fire only if we have no alternative.'

The car slewed, the soft soil tearing beneath the multiple wheels, and suddenly came straight at them. Lanson grunted, trying to watch and to keep hidden at the same time. The tang of hot oil hung heavily on the misty air, and his skin prickled at the thought of the unshielded radiation pouring from the engine room.

Bender gasped, and lunged as if trying to get to his feet. Lanson caught him, held him by sheer force. 'Wait,' he gasped. 'Wait until the last moment!'

Above them the patrol car lurched and swayed with increased speed, the broad wheels tearing the ground on a path that would take them directly across the spot where the two men hugged the dirt.

Desperately they rolled. A metal-edged tire scraped Lanson's back, almost crushing his arm, then he was free and staring up at the metal flooring of the low-slung vehicle. Rods studded it, control rods, handholds for maintenance workers, the raised edges of hatches and the ribbed metal of girders. He lunged upwards, his hands slipping on the oily metal, then he gripped, his feet dragging on the ground. A twist of his body, a tearing effort of back and leg muscles, and he rode beneath the underside of the vehicle, his hands on a brace rod, his feet resting on a shock absorber dangerously near to the churning wheels.

Bender grinned at him from a similar position.

'This car must return to the city,' yelled Lanson above the noise of the engines. 'If we ride it in, it will be safer than chancing our luck on foot.'

Bender nodded, his lips framing a single word. 'When?'

Lanson shook his head, then concentrated on hanging on against the lurching of the speeding of the patrol car.

Life became an unrelenting effort to keep a grip on oil-covered metal, to keep feet balanced on a narrow support inches from spinning wheels that would crush a leg or tear off a foot without loss of revolution. The jolting of the vehicle brought on motion sickness, and limply they hung on and prayed for the patrol car to stop. When it did, Lanson dropped weakly to the ground, tugging at Bender's sleeve and trying not to cry out with the pain of returning circulation. Above them, the car hissed, thin wisps of steam jetting from orifices between the wheels.

'Are we there?' whispered Bender. Lanson squinted towards the front of the car.

'I think so. There is a road, and what seems to be an assembly point. We're past it; this car must be on check-point duty.' Stiffly he crawled towards the rear of the vehicle. 'If we can sneak out unobserved, we can walk into the city without answering a lot of questions. Ready?'

Bender nodded, and together they slipped from beneath the car. It was small for a city, as they remembered the huge metropolis of their own world. It seemed new, with slender tapering spires and graceful buildings. People moved between them, men and women, dressed either in sober brown, or in the gaudy red and green they had seen before. A group was assembled just behind them, and the uniformed crew of the patrol car was busy checking the identification of the civilians. An officer looked at them, frowned, opened his mouth as if to shout an order, then shrugged and resumed watching the group before him. Lanson sighed with relief.

'We did it,' he said as they entered the built up area. 'They're obviously checking all entrants to the city. We were lucky.'

'Yes,' agreed Bender absently. He looked at the buildings, and at the people thronging the wide streets. They were mostly young, well developed and healthy-looking men and women. There were no children, and very few old people.

All seemed busy. All had an intent expression, and all seemed extremely contented. A few red and green uniformed officials moved about the streets, or directed small vehicles at traffic crossings. No advertisements littered the clean newness of the buildings, and the shops were full of odd items of wearing apparel, books, and even thick barrelled weapons.

'This is different to what I expected,' muttered Bender. 'These people don't look as if they have been conquered and are slaves.' He licked his lips at the sight of a restaurant. 'How about food, Lanson? I'm hungry.'

'A good idea,' agreed Lanson. 'Marvin gave me some money, enough for a meal at least. We'll eat, then look for the contact of the Free People.' They swung into a brightly lit restaurant.

A girl smiled at them as they entered, and ushered them to a booth. 'What would you like, sir?'

'Steak.' said Bender smacking his lips. 'Rare, and with mushrooms, fried potatoes, green peas, and lots of onions. Then I'll have cheese, coffee, and finish off with brandy.'

'I'm afraid I don't understand you, sir.' The girl frowned. She was young, with a delicate complexion unmarred by any trace of cosmetics, and Bender smiled as he stared into her eyes. Lanson coughed.

'What have you, miss?'

'Soya soup, energised, of course. Vitaminised protein, whole bread, yeast patties, synthetic vegetable tissue and naturally water.'

'Bring two balanced meals,' ordered Lanson. 'I'll leave the choice to you.' He frowned at Bender. 'Be careful will you? We don't know how much the mode of these people has altered. They seem to be strictly vegetarian, and synthetic vegetarians at that.'

'She looks nice,' said the youthful Bender enthusiastically. 'I wonder if she'd come out tonight?'

Lanson snorted and stared out of the window.

The food seemed tasteless, but extremely filling. Lanson reached for his cigarettes after the meal, then remembered Marvin's comment and decided not to smoke. He had very few left anyway, and there was little chance of getting more.

Apart from themselves the restaurant was empty, and he called the young waitress across to the table.

'Yes, sir?'

'Are you usually this quiet?'

'How do you mean, sir?'

'Well, is business always this poor?'

She frowned, then smiled in understanding. 'You must be new arrivals to Zytlen. The workers are fed at the factories, of course, and we won't get busy until later on.'

'I see.' Lanson took some of the money Marvin had given him from his pocket. 'What do I owe you?'

'Ten credits, sir.'

'Take it, will you.' He offered her the money in his hand. She stared, then looked at him with sudden suspicion.

'This is outdated, sir. I want ten labour credits of the current period.'

'This is all I have, isn't it any use to you?'

'No. All credits are changed regularly, and you have some of the old issue.' She was no longer friendly.

'Look.' Lanson stripped off his wristwatch. 'Will you take this in exchange? I'll come back for it when I have some money.'

'I can't do that. I must insist on the correct credits.'

'Don't be awkward,' snapped Lanson. His mouth tightened. became suddenly cruel. 'Take it, or get nothing.'

'I know what you are,' she said. Her eyes widened, and before they could stop her she had run to the open door. 'Help!' she screamed. 'Police! Help!'

'Let's get out of here,' snapped Lanson.

'Labour drones!' the waitress screamed. 'Police! Police!'

A vehicle slid to a stop outside the restaurant, a small edition of the huge patrol cars. Steam hissed and a door swung open. A red and green uniformed offical sprang from the car, a thick barrelled weapon in his hand.

'What's the trouble?'

'In there, officer. Labour drones; they tried to force me to accept old tokens, and even offered me barter.'

'Did they?' The offical smiled grimly. 'We'll see about that.' He stepped inside the restaurant door.

Lanson struck him once with the butt of his flare gun. As the policeman fell, he snatched the weapon from his hand, pushed aside the waitress, and with

Bender at his heels, raced down the street. Behind him the young girl shrieked at the top of her lungs. Whistles blew, more cars began to gather. Suddenly the area was full of police.

6

The trial

Lanson jerked to a halt, his eyes darting over the advancing figures of the brightly uniformed police. They blocked the street before them, more came from the rear, while others seemed to spring from every building. The civilians moved quietly away, vanishing into buildings or sidling to the edges of the pavement. The whole thing seemed like a well-rehearsed manoeuvre, and within seconds Bender and he were alone, conspicuous in their brown clothing among the red and green uniforms.

'What next?' gasped Bender.

'In here,' snapped Lanson. He led the way towards a building, thrusting aside the few civilians in their path. A policeman lunged forward, threatening them with his pistol. He staggered, then fell heavily as a middle-aged man casually tripped him. The man winked, and gestured with his thumb towards a half-concealed door.

Lanson nodded, tugged the door open and thrust Bender through it. He glanced around for their savior, but the man had lost himself in the crowd. A shot boomed from the direction of the wide doors, and something smacked against the wall scant inches from Lanson's arm. Hastily he slammed the door, and raced down a narrow passage.

'Where to from here?' Bender wiped the sweat from his face and neck.

'Listen,' snapped Lanson. He thrust his flare gun into the younger man's hand. 'I'm going to draw off pursuit, but in case I'm captured, take this. You know the address of the man we're supposed to contact. Get there. I'll try and join you later, but if I can't make it, don't worry. Just do the best you can; and, Bender — '

'Yes?'

'Don't cut lose with the flare guns. We have friends here and you may do damage.' Lanson listened to the growing sounds of pursuit as the door yielded to violent blows. 'Get moving.'

He waited until the door crashed, then deliberately fired his captured weapon at the advancing police. He aimed high, the ball smacking against the roof, then flung the empty pistol at the nearest pursuer. The man ducked, then raised his own pistol.

'Halt!' he called. 'Halt, or I fire!'

Lanson grinned, and darted down a side passage. Within a few minutes he was hopelessly lost, but he had drawn the police from Bender's trail.

A door in the passageway led into a room cluttered with desks and filing cabinets. A girl screamed at him, then flung a paperweight. He slipped from the room, into another crammed with dusty tomes, then back into a wide passage. Red and green moved towards him, and he turned and ran the other way. A pistol thundered. Another. Something hummed past his ear, then all the stars of the universe blazed before his eyes. He was unconscious before he hit the floor.

His head ached and his bones felt like water. He groaned and carefully touched the side of his head. It felt wet, and he stared stupidly at his blood-stained fingers. A boot thudded into his ribs.

'Get up.'

'Wait a minute. I — '

The boot swung again. 'Get up, drone.'

Weakly he staggered to his feet, clutching at the wall for support. Red and green swam before him, mingled with a blur of white faces and gold insignia. A hand steadied him, and a voice echoed as if from far away.

'He's pretty bad, sir. Shall I call a car?'

'No. If he can't walk, we'll carry him.' The voice sounded grimly amused. 'Can you walk?'

'I'm not sure. I — '

'Walk if you can,' urged the first voice. 'If we have to carry you, it'll be feet first — with your head banging. Well?'

'I'll walk,' promised Lanson.

'Good. Steady now.'

Slowly his vision cleared, the throbbing agony in his head easing a little. They were out of the building now, a burly policeman supporting him as he lurched along.

'Where's your friend?' he whispered.

Lanson looked blank, 'What friend?'

The man grinned, and gave a brief nod. 'Stick to that,' he whispered. 'What was the trouble?'

'No money.'

'That's bad. Drones aren't welcome, you'll have to go before the Zytlen court.'

'What's that?'

'Don't you know?' The man looked at him suspiciously, and Lanson knew that he had made a mistake. He groaned, almost falling and staggering so that the policeman had to use both hands to keep him upright. He never noticed the loss of his pistol. The expression on his face when he felt the barrel dig into his ribs made Lanson feel a lot better.

'You'll never get away with it,' the man snarled. 'Give me the gun.'

'No, and you needn't worry about me getting away with it.' Lanson smiled grimly. 'I could like you, friend, but you know a little too much for my health.' The man began to sweat as he saw his prisoner's intention.

'Don't,' he gasped. 'Don't. I — ' The

hand gripping Lanson's arm twitched in a peculiar way, and the appeal in the policeman's eyes was unmistakable. Lanson grinned and returned the weapon.

'That's all I wanted to know,' he said quietly. 'Thanks.'

The man was one of the Free People. Lanson had found a friend.

The formalities were few and soon over. The young waitress filed the complaint. The policeman Lanson had struck gave evidence, and all that remained was for sentence to be passed. Lanson was thrust into a cell with three others to await his turn to appear before the Judge, and tried to make sense of the new scheme of trying criminals.

The accusers didn't appear with the accused. Their evidence was taken separately, the trial was strictly between the prisoner, the sworn testimony and the Zytlen Judge. It seemed efficient, it saved any wasted time, but it didn't seem very much like justice.

A man sidled across the cell and sat down beside Lanson. He was a furtive looking creature, with an old-young face and cunning eyes. His breath stank, and he could have done with a bath.

'What's the matter, friend? In trouble?'

'Aren't you?' Lanson tried not to show his contempt.

'Maybe, and then again, maybe not.' The man leered 'There's always ways of getting out of it.'

'How?'

'Ways,' the man said vaguely. He squinted at the tall man. 'You're a hick, ain't you? I can always tell a yokel. Just off the farm, friend?'

'Yes.'

'You're lucky.' He dropped his voice. 'Your folks would be worried if they knew you were in trouble, wouldn't they?'

'Yes.'

'I can get you out of it. I got friends.' He winked. 'Now if you was to give me a note to your people, just a few lines ordering them to give me something, a chicken say, or a few dozen eggs — ' He let the suggestion trail off into silence. Lanson looked down at the rat-like features.

'What are you, an agent provocateur?'

'A what?'

'A trouble-maker, a spy.' He gripped the front of the man's greasy jacket. 'What are you after, blackmail?'

'No. Honest I'm not.'

'Get away from me.' Lanson flung the little man across the cell. 'Scum like you should be shot.' He grinned to himself at the man's expression. He was pretty certain what the man was. Police methods didn't seem to have changed as much as other things in the past thirty years.

Time wore on, the day died, and the cell began to fill with darkness. Footsteps on the stone corridor signalled the arrival of the guards, and the cell door swung open. Lanson, together with the three other men, filed into the corridor, then into a waiting room. The little man went first, wriggling in the grip of his guard, then one of the others, then Lanson followed him.

The courtroom was surprisingly small. A table supporting an enigmatic machine; two men sitting at the table; a slightly raised dais with a wide desk; a chair behind the desk, and on the chair — a Zytlen.

Lanson felt sick. He swallowed, tried not to look, tried to appear indifferent, casual, normal, but he couldn't do it. For the Star People were not human.

It squatted, toad-like, with masses of bulging mottled flesh oozing with moisture and heavy with a redolent odour. Thin, whip-like tentacles sprouted from the gross body, with thicker ones that must have supported its weight, when moving. The head was a nightmare, with a great gash of a mouth, and protruding eyes. It was alien and obscene. It spoke in a deep guttural voice, and used perfect English.

'What is the charge?'

'Labour drone, Exalted.'

'The evidence?'

'Ordered and ate food worth ten labour credits. Offered out-of-date tokens as payment, then an item of personal property as barter. Accused also made a threat, assaulted a police officer, fired a pistol at an officer with murderous intent, and tried to escape arrest.'

'Is this true?'

'Yes.' Lanson was eager to get this over. He felt ill, his head throbbing with pain from the wound, and he didn't want Bender to be brought into it.

'There is something strange here.' The alien stared emotionlessly with its ophidian eyes. 'This man does not seem to realise the seriousness of what he has done, also he is lacking in respect to one of the Super Race.'

'I meant no disrespect Your Exalted,' stammered Lanson hastily. 'I am but newly arrived to the city, and as yet your ways are strange. My crime, if it was a crime, was wholly unintentional, and I plead for leniency.'

'The Zytlen are always lenient with their children,' boomed the deep voice. 'We have a high regard for the men of Earth, and we permit them many liberties. We train them, guide their economy, weed out the unfit. It is the duty of the Star People to build a new and finer race of Earthmen, so that they themselves may take their place among the peoples of the stars.'

'Yes, Your Exalted.'

'Men must work, for there can be no place for idlers and drones. To avoid work is a crime, to seek to rest while others labour is a thing to be stamped out. We of the Zytlen have great plans for the men of Earth, but before they are fit for their great destiny, they must work and pay for their terrible crime in combatting the Star People.'

Lanson stared at the floor, saying nothing.

'To atone for your crime, you must work as directed.' The alien turned his repulsive head towards one of the two men sitting beside the strange machine. 'Have we need of engine room crew for the patrol cars?'

The man pressed a button, and stared at the flickering sheets of an automatic file 'No, Your Exalted.'

'A pity. It would be an honour for you to assist in patrolling our area.'

'No thanks.' gritted Lanson. He swayed a little, feeling strangely lightheaded and careless. The obscene form of the alien blurred and seemed to writhe before his dimming vision. A guard gripped his arm, and the sting of his open handed slap helped to clear his head.

'What did you say?'

'I said that I am not worthy of the honour, Your Exalted.'

'I see.' The cold round eyes stared emotionlessly at the tall figure of the prisoner. 'It seems that you know little of the Zytlen, and even less of your duty towards them.'

'I crave your forgiveness, Exalted.' Lanson gestured towards his temple, where the blood still oozed from his wound. 'I have been shot, and am not in full possession of my senses. If my remarks seem to be other than what I intend, it is this wound that is to blame, not I who have always been grateful that I am living beneath the benevolent auspices of the Star People.'

'Take him to the power rooms of the main tower.' The alien stared at the semi-conscious figure standing before him. 'Place him in a cell until his wound has healed.'

'His sentence, Exalted?' One of the men looked at the alien, his fingers resting on the machine ready to record the verdict.

'Ten years,' boomed the deep voice. 'Remove him.'

Half fainting, Lanson was carried away. He had a confused impression of underground moving belts, of humming machinery, and of long narrow corridors. Several times they halted, and once he felt the sting of a hypodermic in one arm.

He felt numb after that, and seemed to be walking on a mass of soft cloud. His head floated like a balloon and thought drifted through his mind like wraps of fog. He didn't notice the increasing heat of the air, the thick stuffiness of it, and the smell of oil. He didn't notice when the guards stripped off his clothes and dressed him in thick coarse denim. He walked with glazed eyes and a stupid smile, and the wound on his temple made an angry blotch against the waxen whiteness of his skin.

Metal clashed behind him, and he stood alone. Bars surrounded him, gleaming in the brilliant overhead lights, caging him in. He walked forwards, his legs moving to a long forgotten command. Something struck his knees, and he fell heavily to the metal floor. His last impression was of a pale blob of a face peering down at him.

7

The secret ship

The place was a junk shop, a low roofed house nestling at the edge of the newer buildings of the city. The main window was covered with grime, and behind it lay a tumbled heap of clothing, broken pottery, glass, and various objects long since discarded. A thin door opened at a touch, and a bell jangled tinnily. A man arose as Bender walked in.

He was an old man, almost the first Bender had seen in the city. He walked with a pronounced stoop, his back bowed either from age or from some infirmity. He was bald, his naked scalp glistening in the dim light, and his clothes reeked of age. He peered at the blond-headed young man with little shrewd eyes, and unconsciously rubbed his hands.

'Yes, sir?'

Bender swallowed and tried to appear

nonchalant. 'I want a geiger counter,' he said. 'A pre-invasion model.'

'A what, sir?'

'A geiger counter.'

The old man shook his head. 'I'm afraid that I don't know what you mean. What would it be for?'

'A geiger counter is a machine used for detecting the presence of radioactivity.'

'I see.' The old man appeared to be sunk in thought. 'What would you offer for such a machine if I had one?'

'Two thousand and twenty,' murmured Bender. He leaned forward, one hand gripping the butt of a flare gun beneath the shelter of his short jacket. 'Have you one?'

'Are you Lanson?'

'No. Bender.' The young man wiped sweat from his forehead. 'We were separated, Lanson drew off the police who were pursuing us, we were to have met here. Have you seen him?'

'No.'

Bender frowned. 'Are you sure?'

'Yes.' The old man chuckled. 'Marvin radioed news that you were coming, and he seems to have taught you the correct passwords.' He held out a thin claw-like hand. 'My name is Slade, we can dispense with the first names.'

'As you wish.' Bender stared about the interior of the dusty shop. 'What happens now?'

'Wait here. It is possible that your friend may be able to keep his rendez-vous. In any case you must be briefed on conditions in the city. Things have altered since Marvin was here; the Zytlen have tightened their security regulations, and it would be dangerous for you to wander around.'

'We found that out,' Bender said grimly. He told the old man what had happened in the restaurant. Slade shook his head.

'Bad luck,' he muttered. 'You should have had more sense.' He moved quickly across the dusty shop, gesturing for Bender to follow him. 'I'm an institution here,' he explained, 'They tolerate me because I am harmless, and because it gives the fools in the city a false sense of freedom.' He raised a cunningly hidden trap door. A narrow flight of wooden steps led down into darkness. Bender hesitated.

'Where are we going?'

'To a safe place.' Slade impatiently jerked his head towards the steps. 'Go down, I'll lock the door and follow you. Hurry.'

Cautiously Bender trod the narrow wooden steps. He groped blindly at the walls, the flare gun in his hand menacing the area before him. A lock clicked, the trap door banged, and suddenly light blinded him.

A low cellar, its walls made of brick and the roof of concrete, stood before him. Fluorescent lighting glared from gleaming tubes, and benches rested against the dirtpacked floor.

'Not the best hiding place,' Slade explained, 'but it is only one of several. You'll be safe here for a while.' He sat on one of the benches. 'Marvin didn't tell me very much. Why are you here?'

'I'm not too sure,' confessed Bender. 'Lanson is the one you should talk to, he had a plan, but a lot depended on what he would find here.'

'A plan to beat the Zytlen?' Slade jabbed at the dirt floor with the toe of a cracked boot. 'We all have had such plans, but all have had the same end. We can kill the Star People, that's easy, but it isn't enough.' He looked at Bender with his bright little eyes.

'You know of the orbiting space ship?'

'Yes.'

'Then you know what we're up against. If a single Zytlen dies by an Earthman's hand, the entire city would be beamed with their death ray. It happened once.'

'I know. Marvin told us.' Bender leaned forward, his young face intent. 'Lanson knows that, and I feel that he knows how to overcome it. Did Marvin tell you who we are?'

'No. The radio isn't often used, only in case of emergency. Marvin told me to expect two, men, you and Lanson. He didn't tell me more.'

'We are not of your world. I don't know if you can understand it, but we are from an alternative existence, one in which the Zytlen didn't land on Earth. I am an astrogator. I could plot the orbit of the space ship. Lanson is a rocket pilot, he could handle a rocket ship if you had one, and blast the orbiting ship from space. Maybe we can do nothing to help you, but Lanson thought that we could, and he is no fool.'

'Incredible!' Slade stared at the young man, doubt clouding his little eyes. 'Have you proof?'

Silently Bender held out one of the flare guns. Slade took it, and looked at it in puzzled wonder.

'It is a flare gun,' Bender said quietly. 'Invented about ten years ago. It is one of the most formidable hand weapons ever devised. With it, Lanson destroyed one of the patrol cars. With it, I could blast my way out of this city. Have you anything like it here?'

'No.' Reluctantly Slade handed back the squat flared barrel weapon. 'Have you more of them?'

'I have two, and thirty extra charges for each weapon. Marvin has four more, and two hundred charges.'

Slowly Slade shook his head. 'Not

enough. Even if it were, there is still the death beam, and we know of no defense against it.' He rose and began striding about the low cellar. 'For thirty years I have worked and hoped for a miracle, something to blast Earth free for ever of the misrule of the Star People. A few more years and it will be too late. One more generation and Earth will be the willing slave of as hideous a race as ever was spawned.' He stopped, breathing deeply, little spots of red showing on his sallow cheeks.

'I saw it all, Bender. I saw the first landing, the insane heroism of our people, the ghastly slaughter. I've seen the race of man fall more and more beneath the domination of the Zytlen. Now the younger people almost worship them. When we old ones are dead, there will be no more of the Free People.' He smashed the thin fist of one hand into the palm of the other.

'Rather than see that day, Bender, I'd be willing to give the word and wipe the Zytlen from the face of the Earth. Then let them beam us, let them destroy every living thing, and leave Earth a lifeless cinder. Better that, than what the toad-like scum intend.'

'What is that?' Bender stared, a little awed by the sheer hate in the old man's voice.

'They are training us, Bender. They are weeding us out, guiding our thoughts, moulding the race of man to their own pattern. We are slaves, willing subjects, food for their mad dreams of conquest.' He laughed curtly at the startled expression on Bender's face.

'For thirty years I've watched and spied, worked and lived a lie. For thirty years I've wondered, but now I'm certain, now I know. The Zytlen are few. Long lived as they are, they can well afford to wait several generations if necessary, wait until they have a hundred million willing slaves. Soldiers, Bender! Cannon fodder! Crews for the space ships they are secretly building. An army of humans to be the spearhead for further conquests. Other fair worlds to be the slave camps of the Zytlen. We'd be better off dead!'

'Space ships!' Bender gripped the old

man by the thin arm. 'What do you mean?'

'What I say.' Slade sank back to the bench. He was breathing heavily, and he clutched weakly at his heart.

'The factories are working day and night. Every effort is channelled into continuous production, even food is secondary, that is why the city lives on yeast and synthetics. The workers are building space ships, small fast craft obviously designed for attack. They don't know what they are building. This work is broken down into separate units, but there can be no doubt the Zytlen have stockpiled enormous supplies of partly completed space ships. Hulls in one place, weapons in another, rocket drives in yet a third. This generation is building them, Bender. The next will be trained to operate them, and Earth will be stripped of everything we hold sacred.'

'I can't believe it.' Bender stared at the old man. 'Surely the people know what the Zytlen are doing. Why do they stand for it? Why don't they escape into the woods, refuse to work, anything?'

'How can they?' Slade sounded grimly amused. 'The human race has one terrible handicap, it has been proved often in the past, and even knowing of it, we can do nothing. We are wide open to propaganda. We believe what we are told, providing we are told often enough. The Zytlen aren't stupid, and they studied Earth well before they landed. For thirty years they have drilled into the minds of the young, drilled into the minds of every man, woman and child beneath their control, one simple thing. The Zytlen are benevolent. The Zytlen are eager to help us, after we have purged our crime of resisting their invasion. Now the young people regard their conquerors as benevolent fathers. Superior beings to be obeyed and followed. Speak against the Star People in the public squares, and you would be torn apart by the very people you are trying to help.'

'Then how have you managed to build up your organisation?' Bender asked shrewdly. Slade sighed and shook his head.

'There you have it. The Free People are

the remnants of those who remember a time before the invasion. The older people, those of forty or more. Everyone who dies, is killed, or who just vanishes, weakens our strength, and we can't replace them, Bender. We cannot recruit more members, and our time is running out.'

A buzzer sounded from one corner of the cellar. Slade looked up, then rose slowly to his feet

'I must go upstairs now. I should be serving in the shop. Stay here, get some rest if you can.' He pointed towards a tall cupboard. 'There is food and drink, but use it sparingly, it is not easy to obtain.'

He snapped off the light, and his feet whispered softly up the stairs. The light came on again after the trap door had closed. Bender stretched, yawned, and went across to the cupboard. The food consisted of a gray hard paste, looking something like cold thick oatmeal porridge, and the drink was water. Disconsolately he ate the tasteless paste, and sipped at the stale liquid. He began to feel worried. Lanson should have been here by now.

Abruptly the lights went out, and

footsteps clattered on the wooden stairs. Bender crouched, the flare gun heavy to his hand, the squat flared muzzle pointing towards the echoing footsteps. A man coughed, and Slade's voice whispered through the darkness.

'All right, Bender. Friends.'

The light snapped on, and Bender stared incredulously at a man dressed in the red and green of the police. His hand darted beneath his jacket, reappeared with a flare gun.

'You're covered.' he snapped. 'Get his gun, Slade.'

'Wait a minute!' The old man squeezed past the immobile officer. 'This man is a friend, Bender. Put away your weapon.'

'Are you sure?'

'Of course I'm sure,' Slade snapped irritably. 'He has brought serious news.' He turned to the officer. 'Tell him.'

'I was one of the men who captured your friend. He has been wounded; a shot grazed the side of his head and stunned him. I helped him all I could, and almost got killed for my trouble.' The man grinned sheepishly. 'He drew my gun and was going to kill me. He must have been a little frightened, and it's lucky for you both that I was the one with him. I managed to give him the sign of the Free People. He understood it, and fortunately for me the officer in command didn't notice anything unusual.'

'Well?' snapped Bender harshly. 'What happened to him?'

'He was taken before the Zytlen court, there was no alternative, labour drones always are. I know a guard who was with him when he was sentenced, and I came here to pass on the information as soon as I could.'

'Yes?'

'The toad was suspicious, but must have been careless because he didn't order the lie detector, nor did he order torture.'

'Get on with it,' snarled Bender. 'What happened?'

'Lanson got sentenced to ten years in the main power rooms.'

'Ten years!' Bender slumped back on the bench. 'Are you sure?'

'Yes.' The uniformed man shifted his feet restlessly.

'There's one good thing, you weren't mentioned. Someone forgot to report that there had been two men at the restaurant.' He looked at Slade. 'I'd better go now, they'll be missing me if I stay away too long.'

Silently Slade led the way up the narrow staircase, the light snapped out, the trap door thudded back into place, and heavy feet moved across the ceiling. Bender sat where he was, his youthful face set into grim lines, staring into the darkness.

He was still sitting that way when Slade returned.

'That alters things,' said the old man.

'Does it?'

'Yes. We can't rely on Lanson now. I know all about the main power rooms.'

'You don't know Lanson,' said Bender in a voice that sounded strange to the old man. He stirred, then looked down at his hands. He was holding a flare gun in each.

'I'll get him out if I have to burn this rotten city to the ground. I'll blast him free, and kill anyone or anything that tries to stop me. Ten years! Ten years of hell, I won't stand for it!'

'You can't do anything,' protested Slade. 'You don't know what you're up against. The Zytlen, their police, the whole population. You'd never make it, and even if you did, remember the death beam.'

'To hell with all that,' snarled Bender. 'Lanson is my friend. He's saved my life, and I know that he'd save it again. If I'd been caught do you think he wouldn't have rescued me? Of course he would. I know him. I've fought with him, and when you fight next to a man you get to know him pretty well. I'm going to get him out of there.'

'Wait!' pleaded the old man.

Bender stood upright, his blond curls almost touching the roof. 'That's been your trouble too long. Wait! For thirty years you have waited, and for what? To rot in a crummy hideout saving your skins while better men died. You've waited for so long that you're afraid to move.'

'Maybe you're right.' Slade sagged back onto the bench and rested his head in his hands. Suddenly he looked tired and old.

'It hurts,' he whispered, 'but then the truth sometimes does. I've grown too old, too cautious. I've sat and watched my race, my world, gradually decline into serfdom, and I've waited. I've waited for a miracle, and forgot that miracles happen only when they are made to happen. We all have been content to wait.'

'You will rescue Lanson?'

Bender looked up at the old man, surprised by the sudden virile energy blazing from his eyes.

'Yes.'

'How can you do that?'

'We can do it, but to be successful planning will be necessary. Lanson must stay where he is for a while, but it will not be for long.'

'Then what?'

'We shall see.' Slade smiled at the young man. 'To work. First you must plot the course and orbit of the alien space ship. I'll leave the details to you, I know nothing of such things.'

'I can plot the orbit, if you will give me an idea of its size.' Bender grinned and thrust the flare guns beneath his jacket. 'Then what?'

'I have a secret,' confessed the old man. 'I've kept it to myself, mostly because of caution, but partly because of pride.'

'A secret?' Bender frowned.

'I know where there is a space ship,' whispered Slade. 'An old ship, one built just before the Star People landed.'

8

Escape

Pain flooded him, the pain of neglected wounds, sore muscles and the bitterest pain of all, that of defeat. Lanson groaned, and opened his eyes. He felt stiff and sore, and beneath him he could feel the chill of metal. Painfully he climbed to his feet.

A man grinned at him, a wizened little runt of a man, with thin white hair and a seamed monkey-like face. He smiled and nodded, then ran forward to support Lanson as he staggered towards a bare wooden bunk.

'Take it easy, there's plenty of time.'

'Where is this?' croaked Lanson. 'What am I doing here?'

'This is the annex to the main power rooms of Zytlen.' The little old man peered at the tall adventurer. 'Wait a minute. I'll get you some water.' He stepped across to the bars of the cage and rattled them, yelling at the top of his cracked voice.

'Help! Quick! Help I say!'

A guard came running, then cursed as he saw the old man. 'Quiet down, Pop. Want me to come in there?'

'Get me some water will you?' The old man gestured towards Lanson. 'If you want him to die on you, just forget that I asked, but the toads won't like that, will they?'

'You snivelling rat!' The guard glared his anger. 'Keep a respectful tongue in your head, or I'll come in there and tear it out.' He looked at Lanson. 'Is he bad?'

'Dying.'

'You've had your ration for today,' grumbled the guard.

'Then let him die.' The old man shrugged. 'It will be you that has to do the explaining, not me.'

'Wait,' snapped the guard. He left and returned with a bucket of stale water. 'Here, but if you yell just once more tonight, I'll beat you to a pulp.'

Unlocking a hatch in the barred wall of

the cage, he passed through the bucket, relocking the hatch after the old man had taken it. Gently the old man supported Lanson's head as he drank, the water spilling from the bucket and running down his chin.

'Thanks.' Lanson poured the rest of the water over his head, wincing at its sting on his open wound. He looked at the old man. 'Tell me about it.'

'About what?'

'This.' He gestured towards the iron bars of the cage, the dim lights glowing in the clear area surrounding them. 'Where are we?'

'I told you.' The old man grinned, then stuck out his dirty paw. 'My name is Pop, just Pop. What's yours?'

'Lanson.' He touched his head and winced. 'I had a little trouble, and I remember some fat obscenity telling someone that I had to work for ten years in some main power room. I must have blacked out after that.'

'They probably drugged you,' explained Pop. 'I'll bet you can't remember the journey here.'

Lanson thought for a while, then shook his head. 'No.'

'Neither can anyone else. It makes escape harder when you don't even know where you are.' The old man stared at the tall strong figure beside him on the bunk. 'You look pretty fit, Lanson, but you'll never last ten years, no one ever does.'

'Why not?'

'I don't know.' The old man grinned. 'We work in the power room, tending the fires beneath the steam boilers. The steam is used to drive the turbines, and they drive the dynamos. There's something funny about that engine room. Men get sick there, awfully sick, then they die.' He cackled, rocking on the bunk. 'All except me. I don't die, and I've been here for a long time now.'

'How long?'

'I don't know, but a long, long time. I've seen 'em come and go, come and go, but I never go with 'em.'

'What do you do?'

'I clear up. I load the dead ones and cart them away. Pop, they call me. I've been here a long time.'

Lanson shuddered a little as he looked at the old man. He was half insane, the little eyes in his monkey face glittering with mad amusement. There was something about him not quite normal, a strange irregularity, something more felt than seen.

'How old are you?' asked Lanson.

'How old?' Pop cackled again. 'Guess.'

'Do you remember the invasion?'

'You mean when the toads came? No. I was only a little shaver then, but I remember well enough what happened afterwards.'

'I see.' Incredible though it was this man could not be more than just over thirty years of age, and yet he looked all of sixty. Lanson shuddered, remembering the engine room of the patrol car. Somehow, Pop was naturally immune to the worst effects of radiation, they had aged him beyond belief, but they hadn't killed him. He sighed, resting his throbbing head against the bars of the cage.

He had to escape! To stay here was to die a horrible death. Bender would be waiting for him, and Burges also. Marvin had hoped that he could free the Earth from the heel of the Zytlen, and he had thought so to. He could do nothing while imprisoned. He had to escape!

'What did you say?' The old man, Lanson still couldn't think of him as other than old, leaned towards him.

'I must escape,' whispered Lanson. The cage began to sway before him, the gleaming bars weaving strange patterns before his blurred vision.

'I must escape.'

'Of course you must,' chuckled the old man. 'That's what they all say, but none of them ever do.'

Blackness closed around Lanson, and the sound of the old man's insane laughter.

He went to work the next day. He, Pop, and twenty others from the same cell block. Guards ringed them, their hands ready on the butts of their heavy pistols, and watched constantly as they labored before the stinking heat of the boilers.

The work seemed simple. Lights flashed on a high board as the steam pressure rose or fell. In response they thrust rods into slots before them, thrust them in when the pressure dropped, withdrew them when the pressure rose too high. It was simple, monotonous work, a moron could do it. An automatic device could have done it far easier, but men were cheap.

The slots before them were the openings of a crude atomic pile the rods tipped with fissionable elements. As more and more of the element was placed in close proximity, it reached critical mass, began to fission, spitting off showers of neutrons which in turn smashed into the atoms of the element and gave off yet more neutrons. It was a chain reaction of a low order of efficiency, simple, easy, and utterly fatal to the men controlling it.

Alpha, beta and gamma rays sprayed the area. The neutrons were absorbed by the water surrounding the pile, and as they were absorbed, yielded their incredible energy in the form of heat. The water boiled, turned into steam and spun the huge turbines, then was condensed and pumped back into the water-jacket around the pile.

The by-products of the fission, the alpha, beta, and gamma rays, sprayed from the poorly-shielded pile, riddled the entire area and poisoned every living thing within range with radiation.

It was a death trap. The water, the turbines, the metal of the pumping gear, the connecting rods and gears between the turbines and the dynamos, the metal of the walls, the roof, the floor, all were loaded with lethal radioactivity. The place was 'hot' in more ways than one.

The guards didn't seem to know of the radioactivity. The prisoners didn't seem to know what it was that seared their flesh, made them tired and listless, and caused their blunt nails to continually scratch at their tender skin. They worked dumbly, leaning against poisoned metal, drinking poisoned water, dull eyed, indifferent, careless of the whips of the guards, and of the shouted threats.

Lanson knew and was filled with a terrible desperation. He had to get out of this place. He could stand a little of the pervading radiation. A few days of it at most, providing he rested between shifts and providing the shifts weren't too long. Thirsty though he was, he dared not drink the water slopping in a dirty bucket. He forced himself not to lean against the warm metal, standing wide-legged, swaying, trying to ignore the throbbing of the wound in his temple.

Time crawled slowly past. Whips lashed at his naked back, and the guards yelled themselves hoarse as they tried to speed him up. He snarled at them, blood trickling down his chin from bitten lips, and ignored their shouted commands. After a long while the shift was over, and they were herded back into their cells.

A bucket of water, and a mound of a grey paste-like substance waited in each cell. Greedily Lanson gulped at the stale water, hoping that it hadn't come from anywhere near the power room, he lowered the bucket and the old man leered at him.

'Still hoping, son?'

'Hoping for what?'

'To escape — or have you thought better of it?'

'No.' Lanson snatched some of the grey paste from out of the old man's monkey-like hands. It was tasteless, but he forced himself to eat. Vitamins were essential if he hoped to stave off radiation sickness.

'You won't escape,' said the old man. He spoke sadly, shaking his head. 'You'll be like all the others, talk a lot to start with, then forget all about it.'

'Could you escape?' Lanson glared at the wizened little figure before him.

'Me?' Pop cackled. 'Easily, if I wanted to, but I don't.' He sniggered, folding his scrawny arms around his hairless body. 'A pity though, it'd be a joke against the toads.'

'You don't like them, do you?'

'No. They spoilt everything for me. I was getting a good living out of the ruins, no-one ever goes there you know, they get sick and die if they do, when the toads caught me.' He glared at Lanson. 'I didn't want to come here. I was happy enough where I was. I had meat to eat, real meat.

Rats, and sometimes a rabbit, good stuff, not this grey slop they give you here.'

'How would you get away?' Lanson tried not to sound too eager.

'I told you. I cart away the dead ones, all I'd have to do would be to duck down the sewers and head for the outside. Easy.'

'Why don't you do it?' urged Lanson. He grinned. 'Think of what the toads would say.' He laughed as if at a great joke. 'It would be better still if you took me with you.'

'How?' The old man glared at him, suddenly suspicious. 'You ain't dead.'

'I could pretend to be. Listen. They know that I've got a bad wound. If I keeled over on the next shift, what would happen?'

'One of the guards would make sure that you're stiff, then I'd cart you away.' Hope gleamed in the little monkey eyes. 'Would you do it?'

'How does the guard tell?'

'What?'

'How does the guard make sure that a

man is really dead?' Lanson amplified patiently.

'It depends. Some of them give a man a few lashes with a whip. Others stick him with a knife, some just kick him a few times.'

'I see.' The radiation would affect the guards as well as their charges. Mental processes would be slowed, the guards would become careless, accepting things at face value. He frowned in sudden thought.

'They change the guards pretty often, don't they?'

'Yes. There's a new shift due soon. Why?'

'We'll do it next shift,' Lanson decided. 'Are you willing to take a chance?'

'I'm not taking any chances,' growled Pop. 'Once the guards give me the signal I don't care if you're dead or alive. I just cart you out, tip you on the refuse heap, then go back to work. It's you that takes the chances.'

'Will you do it then?'

'Sure,' the old man grinned. 'Anything for a joke on the toads.' He curled up on his half of the bunk, still chuckling. Lanson shrugged; he had no alternative but to trust the crazy mutation sleeping beside him, yet it was his only chance. Sleep was a long time coming.

The guards were those who had been on duty the previous shift, lounging against the metal walls watching the prisoners work at the pile. They seemed listless, there were ugly dark blotches beneath their eyes, and they used their whips carelessly, without real force.

Lanson looked at the old man working beside him, then at the watching guards. Several times he swayed on his feet, pressing his hands to his head, and moaning with pretended agony. Twice he fell, and felt the whips of the guards burning into his tender skin, standing the pain for as long as possible before staggering blindly to his feet.

'Now?' whispered the old man.

'Not yet. Wait until the shift is almost over, you know what to do?'

Pop nodded, a grin twisting his ugly features.

Lanson waited as long as he dared. He

gasped, then shrieked with agony, his hands clutching at his temple. He staggered, reeled, then tripped and fell heavily to the metal floor. He twitched once, kicked spasmodically, then lay very still. A voice yelled from above him.

'He's a goner. I knew he wouldn't last, not with that smack he'd got on the head. He was half dead when they brought him here.'

Footsteps moved heavily towards him. 'What's wrong?'

'He's dead I tell you,' repeated Pop. 'I saw him keel over, it's the real thing this time.'

'We'll see,' promised the guard heavily.

'Whipping him's no good,' cackled the old man. 'He can't feel it.'

A thin lash whined through the air. Fire exploded across Lanson's back, but warned by the old man he had readied himself for the blow. Again the whip lashed at him. Fire tore at him, sending quivers of sheer agony ripping along his nerves, turning the firm flesh of his back into red pulp.

The guard tired at last, and coiled his

whip. 'He's bleeding,' he said suspiciously.

'They all do for a while,' cackled the old man. 'He's dead enough, and even if he isn't, do you want the job of nursing him?'

A boot thudded into Lanson's ribs. 'Look! He didn't move. He'll never pull another rod.'

'Dump him then,' snapped the guard. 'I'll come with you.'

'Sure. I'll be glad of the company, and you can help me push him.'

'Shut your mouth,' snarled the guard. 'Do your own dirty work. Hurry!'

Grunting, Pop lifted the inert figure of Lanson onto a little cart. He pushed the small vehicle across to a locker door and waited impatiently for the guard to open it. Together they trundled the silent figure towards the dumping ground.

Cautiously Lanson opened one eye. His senses reeled, the pain from the whipping had almost rendered him unconscious, but the desperate necessity of keeping alert had steeled his nerves. He knew that he would never have a second chance.

They were moving down a narrow corridor, Pop pushing the little cart, and the guard keeping a step in the rear. The old man stopped, and pointed towards a trap door set flush in the metal flooring.

'Lift it for me will you, my back ain't as strong as yours.'

'Do your own work,' sneered the guard. 'Any more of your lip, and you'll join that scum in the cart.'

The old man tugged at the trap, his little monkey eyes burning with hate. He wheezed, then lugged the thick door up on its hinges. A foul odor came welling out of the open trap, an odour of death, and the slime of decay. Curiously the guard peered into the noisome depths, wrinkling his nose with disgust.

'Smells, don't it?' Pop came up beside him and pointed with a skinny finger. 'If you look close you can see the glow.'

'Where?' The guard bent over the open trap, squinting his eyes.

'There,' said Pop, and pushed.

The guard yelled, grabbed at the air, and fell through the hole. A squashing sound and a mad slithering told of his efforts to climb out. The old man laughed insanely.

'Take this for company,' he yelled. Tipping Lanson from the cart he flung it through the hole, then slammed down the metal cover. The thick hatch muffled the desperate screams of the unfortunate guard.

Lanson climbed unsteadily to his feet, his body a mass of pain. The old man grabbed his arm, tugging him towards a round disc set in the floor.

'Quick,' he chattered. 'Down into the sewers, before they come.' The disc clanged above them, and water swirled about their hips.

9

A chance for freedom

The place was a ruin, a crumbled mass of shattered concrete, twisted girders, and broken brick. A faint smell hung on the air. Green things grew sparsely from dropped seeds and wind blown spores, but no living thing disturbed the silence.

Bender looked at the tangled wreckage, then at the bent figure of his guide. Slade gestured with a thin hand, bitterness twisting his old features.

'One of many monuments to the Zytlen,' he said. 'A death ray first, then to prevent men from finding anything of value in the city, they atom bombed it.'

'How about the radioactivity?'

'You're safe enough now, aside from traces at the bomb craters, the area has been free of radiation for five years or so.'

'I see.' Bender frowned over the ruins. 'Is the ship here?'

'Yes. I stumbled on it by accident. A freak saved it from utter destruction. The hangars where it was built escaped injury, but were covered with wreckage.'

Slade began to weave between the heaped piles of smashed concrete. Bender followed him, looking distastefully at the poisonous green of the vegetation. A rat, almost as big as a dog and with glowing red eyes, glared at him from beneath a rotting beam, then scuttled off into the thick gloom.

Slade wended his way down past the twisted girders, treading cautiously on ledges of tumbled brick, and testing each foothold before he trusted it with his full weight. It grew darker as they left the surface, shadows clustering around them, thick with displaced dust Bender looked nervously at the tangled mass above him, glinting with the rays of the hidden sun, then hurried to catch up with his guide.

They reached a cleared space of what at one time must have been ground level, and the old man squeezed through a jagged gap in thin metal sheeting. Something long, and curved, and with a subtle symmetry, loomed above them in the dim light.

'There,' said the old man proudly. 'Was I right?'

Bender ran forward, then tripped over a piece of discarded machinery. He was trembling, straining his eyes as he tried to make out the sleek lines of what was undoubtedly a space ship.

'Can't we have some light?' he snapped nervously. 'I can hardly see a thing.'

'It is a space ship. Isn't it?' Slade licked his dry lips, his thin old voice echoing strangely in the vast emptiness of the hangar.

'It could be.' Bender craned his neck, trying to read the markings stenciled on the gleaming hull. 'It certainly looks like one, but what condition is it in?'

'It looks as if it was finished, ready to go.' Slade clutched at the younger man's arm. 'It is ready, isn't it?'

'How can I tell?' Irritably Bender shook off the old man's grasp. 'Everything will have to be checked, the radar, the engines, the fuel supply. Even if it was ready to blast, we'd still have to clear the runway.' He looked helplessly about him. 'The whole thing's impossible! How can we get the ship free? If we could, how are we going to overhaul it?'

'I thought that you could do that,' suggested Slade. 'You and your friends are technicians, aren't you? Naturally we of the Free People will clear the runway.'

'Your faith in us would be amusing if this whole thing wasn't so serious.' Bender looked disgustedly at the old man. 'Do you think that we can do miracles? How am I to get fuel and equipment? Why man, this thing will take weeks to get ready. I'm an astrogator, not a space ship engineer.'

'What of your friend, Burges? Can he help?'

'We can do nothing without him. Get him here as soon as possible, and, Slade . . . '

'Yes?'

'What about Lanson?'

Slade tried to avoid Bender's accusing gaze. 'I've done my best. Before we can even begin to plan Lanson's release, we have to find out where he is. We've checked the main power rooms, and he isn't there. I've got every man possible looking for him, when one of them makes contact, we'll release him. What else can I do?'

'I've some ideas.' grated Bender. 'It's been almost a week now since his arrest, if he isn't found soon, I'm going to look for him, and I'll do my looking with the help of flare guns.'

'I've radioed Marvin.' Slade seemed eager to change the subject. 'He and Burges are on their way here with every man they can find in the woods. They have to be careful, and it will take a little time, but they will be here soon. Is there anything we can do while we're waiting for them?'

'Lots. We must have light, plenty of light. Food, water, tools and equipment. We don't want to have to stop work on the ship for any reason. You'll have to provide the essentials, Burges and I will concentrate on the ship.' He frowned at the old man. 'I'll stay here. You get back to the city and look for Lanson.'

Slade hesitated. 'You promise not to do anything rash?'

'I'll give you some more time, but remember this, Slade. We can't do anything without Lanson. He is the only one of us who can pass this ship as spaceworthy. I can plot the course, and I know quite a bit about radar and remote control apparatus. Burges can check the engines, but Lanson is the only one who knows how the steering gear should operate. He must set the gyroscopes, determine the centre of gravity, adjust the exhaust fins and trim the ship for flight stability. If you try to blast off without him, you'll either drive the ship into the ground, or you won't be able to steer at all.' He looked seriously at the old man.

'I'm not exaggerating, Slade, and remember, we have only the one chance.'

'I'll find him,' promised the old man. He looked at the towering bulk of the gleaming ship as if he were seeing it for the first time. 'Soon now,' he muttered. 'After thirty years of waiting, it seems hard to believe.'

He shook himself, then squeezed

between the torn metal sheets of the hangar. Bender felt suddenly alone. He glanced nervously about the dim emptiness, jumping at a sudden scuttling sound, his hand darting towards his flare guns. A rat scuttled across the littered floor, and he laughed self-consciously as he forced himself to relax.

Some oily waste, lashed with wire to a half-rotten length of wood, made a crude torch. He lit it, squinting through the black smoke, then methodically set to work.

The equipment was in surprisingly good condition. Most of it had been made from alloys, and was free from rust. Bender carefully checked the machine tools, the welding plant, drills, turret lathes, presses, and all the usual equipment to be found in any well-stocked machine shop.

The power belts had either rotted or had been eaten by the rats, the rats had probably done more damage than both the weather and the atom bombing combined, but the belts could easily be replaced. Power was something else.

He paused, squinting in the flickering light from the crude torch, and stared at a huddle of white bones. Some unfortunate technician had been caught by the death beam of the Zytlen, he could expect to find many more such heaps of clean-picked bones. Rats were not delicate eaters.

He tightened his lips at a fresh scuffling from a shadowed corner. Little red flecks gleamed fitfully in the light of the torch, scattering at his threatening gesture, and he frowned in thought. It would be impossible to sleep here. Sooner or later the starved rats would attack.

He looked up at the towering hull of the space ship. A metal ladder ran from one wide fin to the nose. Gripping the torch firmly in one hand, Bender began to climb the ladder, shadows clustering beneath him as the sun swung past the zenith and no longer illuminated the interior of the hangar. The port was unlocked, and gratefully he slid into the control room. It was free of rats, and after closing both the external port and the interior door leading back to the fuel tanks and engine room, he settled himself down on the cold metal floor. Sleep came surprisingly easy.

Burges arrived next day. With him came Marvin and a willing crowd of helpers. Bender set them to work, clearing the hangar, collecting material for torches, and setting up a field camp. Together he and the old physicist examined the space ship.

'I can get the atomic pile working,' mused Burges. 'We can string lights from the ship's power source, and also power for the machine tools. Luckily the ship appears to have been completed, even the fuel tanks are full, but we'll have to replace some of the atomic elements, their half-life was too short to remain effective over thirty years.'

'Can you do that?'

'Given time, yes. I'll breed new elements in the pile. It won't be easy, but I think that I can manage it.' He looked at Bender. 'How are you going to get the ship ready for blast off?'

'I don't know.' Bender looked worried. 'I've been hoping that Lanson would be here to advise us. You know that he was arrested, of course?'

'Marvin told me.' The old physicist bit his lip. 'Will he be safe, Bender?'

'If he isn't someone will suffer for it,' the young man said bitterly, 'and I don't mean the Zytlen.' He bent over a rough chart he had made. 'I think that the easiest way would be to clear the area immediately above the ship. Then when we are ready, we can cut away the roof and blast straight up. Luckily we don't have to worry about damage from the exhaust: as long as we get the ship off the ground the hangar will have served its purpose.'

'Have you checked the circuits?'

'No. I'll need power for that.' He sighed, looking blankly at the metal of the hull. 'It all comes back to the need for power. Without it we can do nothing. If we hope to hit the Zytlen's space ship, the orbit will have to be calculated to five decimal places. That means I'll need the electronic computer, and the radar control must be exact to within one-hundredth second of reaction time. If it hadn't been for the rats, I wouldn't worry so much, but the chances are that they've gnawed off most of the insulation, if they haven't their very droppings make a potential hazard.'

'Did they get into the ship?'

'I don't think so, at least I haven't seen any, but we can't take anything for granted. If this effort fails, you know what it means to us all.'

'I know,' said Burges quietly, 'and I'm not happy about it. Three men from a different world, the only ones with any practical knowledge of space flight, together with a space ship made over thirty years ago, and we hope to free the Earth of alien invaders who have had a generation to stabilise their position.'

'I see what you mean,' nodded Bender. 'The odds are hopeless; without Lanson they don't even exist, but we must try all the same. You know that.'

'I know it, and that's what makes it so horrible.' The old man shuddered. 'We are gambling everything on a single throw of the dice. I don't like the responsibility. I don't like it at all.'

Bender grunted, then bent over his wiring charts, a frown creasing his forehead. Above them, the men from the woods toiled at their task of clearing the hangar roof of a mountain of debris. Others moved about the hangar floor, and gradually order emerged.

Days passed. Days and nights of sweating effort, of mind-twisting concentration, compressing into hours the work of weeks, forcing sheer talent to replace the calmness of certain knowledge.

Burges laboured over the compact atomic pile in the bowels of the ship. Tensely he slid rods, performed miracles of atomic engineering, guessing the critical mass of rundown fissionable elements, and adding mass to mass in dangerous disregard to his own safety. The pile was shielded. He didn't fear radiation burns, but too much of one element piled together, and neutrons would blaze from the fissioning elements in a wave of destruction that would wreck the pile, penetrate the shielding, and bring horrible death.

It would be a quick death, but it would

mean the end of all their hopes, the ship would be wrecked beyond repair, and the Zytlen would rule Earth forever. It was a chance, but it was a chance that had to be taken. Grimly the old physicist bent over his work, blind and deaf to everything but his delicate atomic juggling.

Bender forced himself to concentrate on checking the infinite tangle of wiring circuits, trying not to think of the old man bent over the humped bulk of the cold atomic pile. Marvin, his scarred face filmed with sweat and twisted with fatigue, drove his men endlessly as they shifted tons of rubble from the hangar roof.

Strain mounted. Tension seemed to hang quivering in the musty air, and tightening overstrained nerves to snapping point. Men snapped at each other, fighting frayed tempers and ready for battle as a means to ease their irritation. Every man thought of one thing, and one thing only. If the pile didn't work, all other effort would be wasted. The future of Earth rested in the hands of a little old man crouching over a cold mass of metal, and there wasn't anything anyone could do to help him.

A needle kicked on a dial. A filament glowed, died, then glowed again. A fan spun, and a geiger counter clicked a few times, chattered briefly, then settled to a soft harmless clucking. Shadows writhed, then vanished as strung lights blazed in sudden triumph. A pulley turned slowly, then hummed with speed. In seconds the hangar came to life and men looked, breathed, and looked again.

Burges had won! The ship was alive again after thirty years of idleness. Earth still had a chance to regain her lost freedom!

Bender was the first to reach him, but Marvin was a close second. Tenderly the blond young man lifted the bent little figure of the physicist from his hunched position by the atomic pile.

'It's a little cramp,' apologised the physicist. 'Too long in one position, I'm afraid that I can't move.' His thin lined faced twisted with sudden agony from his cramped limbs.

'Help me carry him upstairs,' snapped

Bender. 'He needs warmth, hot food, rest.' He looked fondly at the little figure in his arms. 'You did it, Burges. You did it all alone.'

'Thanks, but I shouldn't have taken so long.' Burges grinned, then slumped heavily in Bender's arms.

'Exhausted,' Bender explained. 'He's passed out with pain and fatigue. A good thing, too; that cramp must be giving him hell. He'll be as good as new when he's had a sleep.'

Gently they carried the unconscious man from the interior of the ship, laying him on a pile of blankets near a softly whirling fan. Bender straightened, and stared at the men clustered around the sleeping physicist

'Back to work men,' he ordered. 'Blanket out every crack and hole in the hangar. No light must be allowed to escape, we don't want visitors.'

The men grinned and began to break away from the cluster, new hope shining from tired eyes. Suddenly all sound died. A man stood just within the hangar, a strange man, almost naked, with hot glittering eyes staring from a mat of beard, and a tangle of gnarled black hair. Filth covered him, and his flesh was scarred. He reeled, and held out one hand.

'Give me a gun,' he croaked. 'Give me a gun.'

10

Lanson's Plan

For three days Lanson raved in delirium, burning with fever and infection from his wounds. Bender nursed him, treating the ugly whip scars with salves from the medical kit found on the ship. Always a man waited beside the sick bed ready to call for assistance at the first sign of a change in the sick man's condition.

Bender sat beside the silent figure of his friend, Burges with him, and stared in wonder at the ravaged features, now cleaned of the filthy mat of beard. Lanson turned, sighed deeply and opened his eyes.

'Give me a gun,' he said.

'Burges!' Bender called to the old physicist. 'Quick. He's awake and the fever's broken.' He smiled at Lanson. 'Take it easy now, you're among friends.'

'Give me a gun,' insisted Lanson

weakly but firmly.

Bender looked at the old physicist.

'Give it to him,' said Burges. He rested the palm of his hand on the sick man's forehead, then felt his pulse. 'The crisis is over, he will be well soon, physically well, that is.'

Bender stared at the old man, then slowly passed a flare gun to Lanson. He snatched it, caressing the squat barrel and flared muzzle, then sighed and smiled at the two men.

'Thanks. I'm not crazy, but they'll never get me alive again. Never.' He shuddered in recollection.

'Was it bad?' whispered Bender.

'It was hell.' Lanson paused, his black eyes dull and lifeless. 'They put me to work tending an unshielded atomic pile. A crazy mutant helped me to escape. Somehow he was immune to the normal effects of unshielded radiation, but they had ruined his mind.'

'We looked for you,' said Bender. 'The Free People that is, they searched for you everywhere.'

'I escaped on the second day.' Lanson

licked his lips and drank greedily of the water Bender passed to him. 'We jumped into the sewers, Pop and I. How long we wandered through those dark wet tunnels, I'll never know. We drank filth, ate refuse, rats, slime. I knew that my wounds had become infected, but there was nothing we could do about it. There were times when I thought that I'd wander forever. How I got out I'll never know.'

He paused, shuddering again at the memory.

'Pop, the old man — though he wasn't old — who helped me escape, found a branch leading off the main sewer. It was probably one that had belonged to the city here, and part of it was blocked by a sagging roof. We had to swim beneath it. I went first, there was nothing else to do. I just made it. Pop didn't. I waited for a long time, I even went back trying to find him, but I couldn't. It was dark, of course, and I could hear the rats squeaking, and the smell of the water was enough to turn a man's stomach. After a long while I continued along the channel, just when or where I left it, I can't remember.'

'How did you find us?'

'I wandered for a long time. Things had grown unreal, sometimes I slept, at others I must have staggered about in a daze. I remember that I saw lights gleaming through the ruins, and tried to get to them. Suddenly I saw men, then I must have collapsed. The next thing I remember is that you were sitting beside me, and I knew that you had guns.'

'Well, you're safe now,' Bender said grimly. 'Marvin is here, and Burges, and they have the other flare guns. If we have to, we'll hold off the entire race of the Zytlen, their human slaves and all.' He gestured towards the towering form of the space ship. 'Slade, the old man we should have contacted in the city, stumbled on this ship a few years ago. We've been trying to get it in working order. Burges has started the pile, and the others have almost cleared the roof. Once we trim the ship for flight stability, we're all set to blast the orbiting space ship from the sky.'

'Good.' Lanson struggled to his feet, sweat beading his haggard features. 'Let's get to work.'

'Rest a while,' protested Bender. 'You're not fit yet.'

'My mind's clear enough, and I can rest later. I want to examine the ship.'

Three days later they held a council of war. Slade was there, Marvin, and others from nearby cities. Lanson, still haggard of feature but otherwise recovered from his illness, dominated the meeting. They sat at a rough table mounted on trestles at the foot of the towering space ship. Guards patrolled the ruins above, and the thin weakened sunlight filled the vast hangar with misty light.

'We are assembled here to discuss the final steps of the plan to rid Earth of the Zytlen.' Lanson stared at each in turn. 'Your comments, suggestions and ideas would be welcome. I think it best to give a summary of the situation as we know it at present. First, the space ship is not quite what we thought it was. Initially it was designed to be a self-contained unit, able to traverse interplanetary space. There are obvious signs of last minute alterations. Radio controls have been fitted, proximity controls and radar steer-adjustments.'

'Wait a minute, Lanson.' Slade held up one thin claw-like hand. 'Remember that we don't all know your technical terms. Those of us that do are hazy as to what they mean.'

'Sorry. I can best explain by saying that this ship has been altered to operate on remote control. In other words, the ship has been turned into a gigantic bomb.'

'What does that mean to us now?' Marvin frowned, his scarred features twisting in the dim light. 'Isn't the ship of any use at all?'

'Yes. Either we can use it for its secondary purpose, a gigantic, radio-controlled bomb, or we can use it as originally intended.' Lanson looked at the intent faces ringing the table. 'The ship is capable of carrying twenty men and women to another planet. With it we can escape Earth, escape the Zytlen, and set up a colony on Mars.'

'Run away you mean?' Marvin spat into the dust.

'You could call it that,' agreed Lanson. 'I'm merely telling you what we can do, it's up to you to decide what we *will* do.'

'I call for a vote.' said Slade. 'For emigration?'

Not a hand rose.

'For attacking the Zytlen?'

He smiled at the unanimous response. 'We can forget about setting up new colonies,' he said quietly.

'Very well.' Lanson looked at a paper in his hand. 'I assume that each of you has made arrangements for a general attack on the Zytlen here on Earth. The attack must coincide with the destruction of their space ship, a little after would be better; in fact we can use the destruction as the signal.' He looked at the circle of faces.

'All this of course depends on their ship being eliminated.'

'Can we be certain that we can destroy their ship?' A stranger asked the question, a thick set, middle-aged man from a different city. Lanson shook his head.

'We can be certain of nothing, but I think that we are safe in basing our plans on certain assumptions. First of all, it's almost certain that they won't have their protective force field operating. It's over thirty years since they needed to use it — at the time of the original invasion — and they no longer fear attack from rockets or guided missiles. We can also assume that there will be a minimum crew aboard their ship. I wouldn't be surprised to find that there aren't any.'

'How can you say that?' protested Slade.

'Logic. The Zytlen haven't had any serious trouble for thirty years, it is natural that they would have relaxed their vigilance by now. Quarters on space ships are notoriously uncomfortable, and they would tend to cut short any time they have to spend on board. As the ship is in a free orbit, no harm could come to it, and they know that we have no weapons capable of damaging it.' He smiled. 'At least we had no weapons capable of damaging it. We have now.'

'How do they get to and from their ship?' Bender looked at the other men. 'Has anyone noticed any other ships ferrying changes of crews?'

'No.' Slade frowned in thought. 'Some of them go on trips, they use the aircraft, and seem to head for the north. I haven't had any reports of ferry craft approaching the space ship, though.'

Lanson nodded and looked at Bender. 'Well?'

'It fits in. Their ship is on a constant variable orbit. By that I mean that it crosses both poles exactly, but orbits the planet in a clockwise direction. It will pass overhead on one orbit, then a hundred miles to the west on the next and so on until it has covered the globe. It will always be above the poles, however, and that would be the obvious place to effect any transfer of crews.'

Lanson smiled at the frowns on the faces of the men at the table 'Look at it this way,' he suggested mildly. 'Think of the Earth as a ball, around this ball is a ring fastened to both poles, the ring is the orbit of the enemy space ship. Now keeping the ring steady, rotate the ball, the path of the ring will circle the ball at a different point at different times. Do you see now?'

They nodded, still not looking too happy.

'Never mind,' said Bender. 'You don't have to worry about that. Your job is to lead the ground forces. What weapons do you expect the Zytlen to use?'

'I'm not too sure.' Slade pursed his lips in doubt. 'They have armed the police and guards with single shot muzzle loading pistols, muskets, too. They're cumbersome, and not of much use in close-quarter fighting. We needn't worry about them. We have weapons equally as good, and trained men to use them. The Star People are something else again.'

'What weapons did they use during the invasion?' He looked at Lanson. 'Remember when we captured the patrol car? You used a flare gun, and the crew babbled about weapons of the Star People. Could they have ray guns, or similar weapons?'

'Possibly,' said Lanson.

'They did use a weapon of some sort of energy beam,' mused Slade. 'A heat gun I'd call it, wide beam, but pretty limited in action. They relied on the space ship and the death ray to conquer Earth.'

'Whatever they have doesn't really matter,' decided Lanson. 'You must place your forces as close to them as possible, then at the signal, cut them down. With any sort of luck at all, you should be able to use their own guns against them. Once the Zytlen are dead, their human guards won't put up much of a struggle.'

He frowned down at the rough table. 'I've a better idea for the signal. We in the ship will keep radio contact, it needn't be anything involved, just a steady signal. When we have smashed their ship, we'll interrupt it, either cut it off, or better still, broadcast a pre-determined code word. You in the cities will receive it, and then fire signal rockets set for low altitude detonation. That way everyone will receive the signal by sight or by sound, and if we do fail to smash the alien space ship, no great harm will have been done by an abortive uprising.'

He looked at the encircling faces. 'You do have signal rockets I suppose?'

'We can get them,' said Marvin. 'I know where they are to be found, and in any case, something could be made to serve the same purpose.' He frowned, moving his finger across the rough table.

'Who will pilot the ship?'

'We shall,' said Bender. 'Who else?'

'I could.' Marvin noticed the surprise on their faces. 'I wasn't always a coward, skulking in the woods. When the aliens came I was a rocket pilot. I knew what it was to ride the heavens on wings of flame.' He touched his scarred features. 'They shot me down, my plane exploded and I was marked for life. At times I wished that I had died when I crashed, at others I was glad to be alive, but I can pilot a rocket ship.'

'No, Marvin.' Lanson leaned across the table, and slowly shook his head. 'You couldn't handle the ship. I know that you have been trained to pilot a rocket plane, but they are not the same. I should know, it took three years of specialized instruction to teach me how to handle those two hundred tons of dead mass. Spaceships aren't rocket planes. The controls are different, the reaction time, the balance.'

He looked at Bender. 'You won't be in the ship, either. Once the preliminaries are attended to, one man can operate it well enough for what is to be done. I shall take the ship up alone. You are needed here, and here you will stay.'

'I'm going,' Bender said stubbornly. 'We've been through too much together for us to part now. Burges must stay behind, he knows that, and so do we, but why should I stay?'

'You realise what it means?'

'Certainly.' Bender smiled, looking startlingly young. 'We're going to die, you and I, but what of it? We are living on borrowed time now, we should have been blasted to atoms in our own world, so what have we to lose?'

From outside a man called a desperate warning. Feet clattered on the thin metal of the roof, and a figure, dust-stained and bedraggled, thrust his way into the hangar.

'Quick!' he yelled. 'Forces from the city are approaching the ruins!'

For a moment turmoil reigned, then Lanson's calm voice forced some degree of order.

'Warn all guards to stay out of sight

Cease all activity. Marvin, you and your men go further into the rubble, and stand ready to attack.'

Tensely they waited.

11

The Zytlen

It was a small group of men in red and green uniforms. They marched in loose formation, weapons at the ready, and with them came a small ground car of the type used for inter-city transport.

Lanson watched them with narrowed eyes. 'I doubt if they know what is here,' he murmured. 'Probably they have noticed undue activity in this area, perhaps they spotted lights at night, in any case they've decided to investigate.'

Bender grunted softly as he eased his position among the rubble. He glanced around him and grinned. Not a soul could be seen, and yet he knew that men lurked behind twisted girders, broken concrete, heaped brick, and all the other debris around them.

'Who has the flare guns?' he whispered.

'We have one each. Burges has one, and

159

Marvin. Slade took one back to the city with him. It is essential that he remains free until the attack. One of the others, the thick set middle-aged one, has the last gun. He seemed to know how to use it.'

'Slade?' Bender looked his surprise. 'Has he gone?'

'Yes. I sent him back as soon as the alarm was given. He is the key man of the Free People; without him, the attack must fail. I won't take any chances on his being recognised.'

'What do you think is in that car?' Bender squinted between two girders. 'I can't see beyond the windows.'

'Probably one of the Zytlen.' Lanson's eyes hardened and he unconsciously tightened his grip on the flare pistol. 'Silence now. Unless they discover the space ship, we do nothing.'

'If they do?'

'We must kill or capture them all, no word of that ship must be allowed to reach others. If we have to shoot, wait for my signal. In the meantime, keep hidden, and wait.'

The sun swung below the horizon, and

the red glow of fires shone among the ruins. The Zytlen had left the shelter of the car, and a tent had been set up on a cleared stretch of ground.

Lanson sent whispered orders back to the waiting men. Half of them crept back into the hangar to snatch food and rest, relieving the others after a few hours. When dawn came, all were back at their posts.

The searching went on. Little groups of the guards poked among the heaps of rubble, spreading out, watching for any signs of activity. The liaison officer moved constantly from party to party, reporting back to the tent each time.

A group of the searchers paused a few feet from where Lanson and Bender crouched in tense silence. Their leader, a thin-featured youth affecting a thin blond moustache, rested his musket against a ledge of stone, and making sure that he could not be seen from the tent, slumped down for a brief rest. The other two quickly followed his example.

'If you ask me this is a waste of time,' the young man grumbled, his words coming clearly to the watching pair. 'If the Star People believe that there is danger in this area, why don't they sterilize it from the space ship?'

'Why should they?' The speaker was a dark complexioned man, heavy built and older than he seemed. 'That takes power, and anyway we're too near the city for the death beam. It would spread, and before we knew it, half of the population would be dead.'

The third man grunted, and fished in his pockets for something, which he stuffed in his mouth.

'What do you think could be happening here?' The young man carefully smoothed his moustache as he asked the question.

The dark man shrugged. 'How do I know? A few discontents, labour drones perhaps, trying to scratch a living from the ruins. Maybe someone looking for something they could sell.' He spat. 'I don't know what the toads are worried about. I notice the one with us isn't doing any sweating.'

'Keep a respectful tongue in your head,' snapped the young man. 'I've noticed you before, and if you're not careful, I'll report you to the Zytlen.'

The dark man yawned. 'Mind you don't strain yourself,' he sneered. 'If you'd served a turn in the power rooms, or the patrol cars, perhaps you'd be less confident of your future. I've seen too many officers die while on guard to worry much what the Zytlen think about me.'

The young man snorted, then reached for his weapon. 'Let's get going, the quicker I get back to town, the better.' He rose, looked casually around, then narrowed his eyes.

'Look! Over there, a cleared space with metal showing beneath it!' He strode forward. 'Call the officer!' he yelled excitedly. 'There's clear signs of activity within this area recently.' He grinned. 'I may get promotion for this.'

The dark man didn't move. Watching him, Lanson was struck with sudden suspicion, and looked at Bender.

'I'll bet the dark one is a member of the Free People,' he whispered.

'He can't help,' Bender whispered back. 'The other man has gone for the officer. Shall we attack?'

'Wait.'

The glittering officer came striding across the heaped rubble, led by the silent third member of the party. He looked at the cleared area, pursing his lips at the exposed roof of the hangar. He bent, rubbed a finger on the metal, and felt the gritty dust.

'Good,' he said, and the young man with the blond moustache glowed at the brief word of praise.

'Do you think this is what the Exalted was looking for?'

'Stay here,' the officer ordered, not replying to the question. 'Keep a sharp lookout. The people who cleared this rubble may still be here. I'll report this to the Zytlen.' He turned away, then stiffened, one hand darting towards the heavy pistol at his belt.

'Don't move!'

Lanson smiled, and gestured with the flare gun in his hand. 'Don't any of you move, and don't shout either. Drop your weapons to the ground.' He waited as the guns were reluctantly tossed down.

'Good. Now take off your clothes.'

'What?'

'You heard me. Undress. Quick now.' He looked at the dark man who had sneered at the Zytlen. The man stared directly at him, then made a curious gesture. Lanson nodded; as he had thought the man was a member of the Free People. 'You too.'

The man started to protest, then thought better of it. Rapidly he stripped off his red and green uniform, and stood shivering in his underwear.

'Are you covering them, Bender?' called Lanson.

'One move and I'll fry them to a crisp,' Bender called back cheerfully. 'What are you going to do, Lanson?'

'You'll see.' Rapidly the tall adventurer changed his ragged clothes for those of the liaison officer. The red and green uniform fitted well and he smiled at his half naked prisoners. 'How do I look?'

'You'd fool me,' grunted the dark man, 'but you'll never get by with that weapon.'

'Thanks.' Lanson slipped the flare gun beneath his tunic, and holstered the thick-barrelled weapon of the officer. Stepping beside the dark man, he muttered low instructions, then stepped back.

'Remember, one move and you'll be dead before you know it. Sit down now, and wait.' He looked at the dark man. 'I trust you to be sensible, if not, you have only yourself to blame.'

With a final look at the squatting men, he turned, strode across the heaped rubble, and deliberately headed for the tent of the Zytlen.

He was not stopped. None of the lounging guards gave him more than a casual glance. They had become used to seeing their officer approach the Zytlen, and it seemed just one of many routine visits. Despite himself, Lanson felt his heart quickening its beat as he neared the tent. Rapidly he thrust aside the thick drapes, and entering, let them fall behind him. An offensive odour welled up and something squat, gross and obscene regarded him from round ophidian eyes.

'Well?' boomed a deep voice. 'What have you to report?'

'The area is clear, Your Exalted.' Lanson kept his head lowered, but he knew that the alien before him could not be deceived. He slipped the flare gun from its hidden holster, and levelled it casually at the alien.

'Don't move!'

Silence thickened inside the tent. Outside the thin voices of men calling to each other echoed across the ruins, seeming very far away. The wide mouth opened, the flabby skin of the toad-like throat pulsed, and suddenly the sickening odour increased.

'What do you want with me?'

'Why did you come here?'

The alien gestured towards the table before him. It was cluttered with maps of the area, sectioned, and marked in red. The Zytlen had conducted the search with an efficiency limited only by the men working with him. Lanson smiled, and deliberately kicked the table aside.

'Answer. This thing in my hand could sear you to charred ash, and it will if you hinder me. Why are you here?'

'Men have entered the area, many men,

and few have left. I wished to discover why.'

'I see.' Lanson looked at the repulsive thing before him. 'Men live here, a few men, but those few are free. We do not wish to live beneath the whips of the Zytlen. Will you leave us alone?'

'Yes.'

'I could kill you, you know that.'

'Yes, but if I die, many men of Earth will die with me.'

'How would your people know that you are dead? We could kill you and then bury you where you could never be found.'

'My people would know.'

'How?'

'They would know.'

'I see.' Lanson looked at the alien with narrowed eyes. 'Telepathy?'

'No. Not mental communication, but they would know.'

'Some sort of rapport then?'

'Yes.' The gross body stirred, the skin with its oozing moisture sending a wave of odour towards Lanson. He guessed that the odour was the thing's way of displaying emotion. The round eyes were as impassive as those of a fish.

'What are you going to do?'

'That depends.' Lanson looked at the alien before him. 'I have many questions I want you to answer, if you answer them, you live, if not — ' He shrugged.

'If you kill me, many Earthmen will die.'

'What of it?' Lanson tightened his lips, looking suddenly hard and cruel. 'What is that to you? If many men die, will that restore your life? Speak, or die!'

The odour grew overpowering. The air within the tent was laden with it.

'What would you know?'

'Good. How many of you are there?'

'Few. We live long but reproduce slowly.'

'Is your space ship manned?'

The Zytlen sat immobile, his round eyes glittering in the subdued light. Lanson repeated the question, then shrugged, he knew that the alien would never answer. He gasped for breath, the atmosphere numbed him, and his head swam. The flare gun almost slipped from his lax fingers. Startled, he tightened his grip.

Still the alien sat immobile staring with big hypnotic eyes.

'What weapons have you?'

'Atomic guns, much the same as the one in your hand.' The booming voice seemed to come from far away. All the world seemed centred in two great ophidian eyes. Lanson irritably shook his head.

'Stop staring at me,' he said thickly. 'Where are you from?'

'A far place. Our vessel was damaged in a war with our own people, and we were cast into deep space. For many years we travelled. We could not return home, our lives were forfeit for past actions. After many years of voyaging we sighted this system.'

'Why did you not come in peace?'

'Peace?' If the alien could have expressed emotion he would have sounded surprised. 'What is peace?'

'Why conquer Earth? Why did you not arrive as friends?'

'What else? We are the superior race, men are — '

'Are what?' Lanson gritted his teeth,

and tried desperately to stop the wavering of the alien before him. 'What are men?'

'Animals,' boomed the deep voice calmly.

With a sudden writhing of tentacles the thing moved. The speed of its motion was shocking, it seemed to flow like water.

Lanson looked sickly up from the ground where he had been flung by a lashing tentacle. His flare gun had fallen from his hand, and he dared not move to regain it. The alien stared at him with impassive eyes.

'Men are fools,' boomed the deep voice. 'You will serve to teach them that fact. We of the Star People have experimented with your race, we have dissected you, found out how your pitifully inefficient metabolism works. It will be interesting to see how long you live with your viscera extruding from your opened body, your brain matter resting on trays. You will live of course, we shall see to that, but those who see you will wish for your death.'

Tentacles writhed as the alien stepped towards the tent flap. Casually it twitched the heavy drapes aside, then spun at Lanson's desperate action.

Fire twinkled from a glistening instrument strapped on one tentacle, cold fire, writhing and twisting as it darted through the air. It sparkled, shimmering with colour, and shrilling with a clear high sound. It touched Lanson.

He screamed, doubling up with agony. Blood poured from lips bitten in helpless reaction, muscles jumped and cramped, senses reeled with pain so utter that it seemed impossible human flesh could bear it and live.

The alien regarded the twitching man with emotionless eyes, then raised the glittering weapon again.

Lanson cringed, rolling on the dirt floor, both hands clutching his middle. He saw the glitter of the alien and with the tattered rags of his strength, forced himself to act.

Fire spat from the recaptured weapon in his hand. The heavy ball smashed into the glittering instrument strapped to the alien's tentacle, a spout of cold fire streamed from it, shimmering twinkling fire, shrilling with a thin high sound, cascading over the writhing body of the Zytlen.

The tent fell, ripped to shreds by lashing tentacles, and smouldering from the fire of the broken weapon. Desperately Lanson rolled across the dirt floor, still doubled with pain, and unable to use his legs. Something hard dug into his side, and he felt the welcome butt of the flare gun.

Outside guards shouted and came racing towards the collapsed tent. A thick booming scream echoed from among the canvas, and the white whips of the lashing tentacles kept the guards cautiously at bay. The booming died, the frenzied lashing stopped. Something heaved, and abruptly the Zytlen stood upright, resting on the thick tentacles studding the lower portion of its gross body.

'Dogs!' it boomed. 'Where is he?'

'Who, Your Exalted?' stammered a guard.

A thin tentacle lashed out, wrapped around the guard's throat, and twitched. Terrible strength lay hidden in that appendage. The guard's body fell in a widening pool of blood, his head torn from his shoulders.

'Where is he?'

'Here, Your Exalted.' The guard pointed at a writhing lump beneath the heaped canvas of the collapsed tent. Eager hands began to pull it away, and soon Lanson stared up at them, his eyes tortured pits in the whiteness of his face.

'Dog!' The alien stared down at him from round, wide eyes. 'I have suffered at your hands. I, a member of the Star People to be injured at the hands of a thing like you.'

Lanson remained silent, his hands still clutched to his middle, his face glistening with sweat A tentacle caressed his face, and blood started to the pale skin. Another whipped across his back, and his body jerked with agony. Slowly and methodically the alien began to beat the helpless figure before him to a blood-stained pulp.

The guards stood silent, their white faces reflecting sick emotion. Whatever their ambition may have been, they were men, and they were watching an alien beat a man to death.

Lanson sobbed, trying desperately to will life into his numb hands. With each lash of the thing's tentacles he could feel life slip away from him, and he had to live. He had to!

The flare gun felt awkward in his hands. The trigger slippery, the whole weapon too heavy to hold. Desperately he pointed it, squeezed the trigger, and fell back senseless.

12

Battle in space

There was a smell in the air, a thick repulsive odour, stinging the nostrils and filling the mouth with saliva. Sharp sounds crackled as if far away, and now and again something thundered, and was followed by thin hysterical screams.

Lanson stirred, licking parched lips, and opening eyes that seemed to have been covered with some sticky substance. His head throbbed, and his back and sides burned with agony. Every muscle ached, and his nerves felt as if they had been scoured with a file.

Something big and gross was beside him. It lay across one arm, and its weight seemed to crush the limb. Flies buzzed, and the stench thickened as Lanson moved. He heaved, pushing the body trapping his arm, and with an effort that left him trembling with weakness, rolled free.

The alien was dead. A great hole charred deep into its body, a hole that oozed thin yellow blood. The camp seemed deserted, the guards scattered, and the sound of battle echoed from the ruins. Lanson staggered to his feet, grimaced at the filthy uniform covering him, and with sudden revulsion stripped it off. He looked for the flare gun, and found it half hidden beneath the sprawling body of the alien.

A shout echoed from the ruins, a scattered cheering, and men suddenly began racing across the ground towards him. Instinctively Lanson raised his weapon, then checked his pressure on the trigger as he recognized the blond-headed Bender.

'Lanson! Thank God that you're still alive. We saw the alien beating you, you fired and fell back and I was afraid that you'd died too. The guards seemed to be stunned, and so we chose that moment to strike. It's all over now.'

'Did any escape?'

'No. I left our prisoners in charge of the

dark man. He's one of us. The rest fought us off for a while, some tried to hole up in the ruins, but the flare guns dug them out.'

'Dead? Wounded?'

'They lost ten men dead, and most of the others are wounded, but not seriously. We lost two men dead, and five slightly wounded.'

'Good.' Lanson kicked absently at the dead alien before him. A cloud of flies lifted on heavy wings and settled again, feeding on the stinking flesh.

'Get everyone to work. The area must be cleared and the ship ready to blast as soon as possible.'

'Yes. We'll do it as soon as we've rested and eaten.'

'No. Do it now. The Zytlen have a rapport between them, they know when one of their number dies. We can expect them over this area in force, and they will use the space ship to sterilize it.' He glanced at Bender.

'How long will it be before their ship is in position to beam us?'

'Unless they change their orbit, and

that won't be easy, several hours yet. They have to spin around the world several times before they get on an orbit from which they could fire on us.'

'Good. That will give them time to evacuate the city, but it will give us time to get the ship into flight trim. We can expect aircraft, of course, and probably ground forces. We must hurry, Bender. Set the guards to work, and kill anyone who hesitates.'

'Right.' The young man looked anxiously at the tall adventurer. 'How about you?'

'I'm all right. I'll be at the ship, there are several things yet to do. Keep guards posted, and let me know the second they see anything approaching. Hurry now!'

He watched the young man hurry away, then moved slowly through the rubble down to the hangar and the ship. Once he stopped and spat blood, wincing and pressing his hand to his ribs. The beating he had taken had left its mark. Several ribs felt as if they were cracked, the muscles of his arm were torn, and he doubted his ability to continue unless he had some rest.

Gratefully he slumped into the padded pilot's chair, and stared at the banked instruments before him. Nostalgia gripped him as he remembered another such ship. A ship built to conquer space, and he, its commander. Sitting in the deep chair, resting his aching body, and letting his gaze drift over the familiar dials and switches, it all seemed very near.

Three years to Mars and back. Three years of plunging through the great emptiness of the void, with stars blazing beacons lighting their path, and the sun a shrinking ball behind them. Mars had proved an arid world, a world of dust and age. They had not stayed long.

Visions swam before him. He felt the quiver of a rocket plane as he flung it over the heavens, the snarl of guns as he blasted the ships of the Logicians from the skies. He was in the strongpoint again, feeling the gentle tremor of the walls that spelt death. Guiding the radio missiles with sure hands, laughing as he felt the rush and surge of emotion, living while he could, certain in the knowledge that he would be a long time dead.

A circle swam before him, misty and strange, limned with fire and fed with the power of the atom. Worlds swirled beyond it, strange worlds and yet each like his own. For a moment he looked into a mirror, and he saw himself in a hundred thousand guises, each the same, and yet each slightly different.

A voice called urgently, and with a start he sat upright in the chair. He rubbed his eyes and looked guiltily about him. For a while he must have been asleep. Sitting there gazing at the instruments, he had dozed and dreamed a little. He shivered with a sudden chill.

'Lanson!' called the voice. 'Where are you?'

'Here,' he answered. 'In the control room of the ship. What's the matter?'

'Planes sighted coming from the direction of the city. Bender sent me to tell you.'

'Right. I'll be with you in a moment.' Painfully he descended the ladder.

Marvin pointed with a finger, his scarred face twisting with emotion. 'Look! Three planes, troop carriers by the size of them. What shall we do?'

'Is the area cleared?'

'Yes. The roof is free of debris, and the ship as finished as we can make it.'

'Then evacuate the area.' Lanson looked at him and grinned. 'Tell all the men to get away from here.'

'What about the planes?'

'I'll see to them. If they are troop carriers we have nothing to fear. If they're bombers, they will fly low to hit their target The Zytlen wouldn't have trained men to drop bombs from a height. In either case I want you and your men away from here.'

Marvin hesitated, his scarred face jerking as he sought for words to express himself. Dumbly he held out his hand, gripped hard, then vanished among the rubble. Lanson could hear his voice as be called sharp orders. He smiled, then turned to watch the oncoming aircraft.

They flew low, strangely slow, huge wide winged machines.

'Sitting ducks,' someone murmured beside him. 'Shall we take off now?'

'Bender! I thought that I told you to go with Burges back to the city?'

'Did you?' The young man smiled, the sun glinting from his blond hair. 'I didn't hear you, and anyway, surely you didn't think I'd leave you to take up the ship alone?'

Lanson grunted, then smiled and slapped the younger man on the shoulder. 'Are you armed?'

'Yes.'

'Good.' Lanson stared at the slow moving aircraft. 'No sense letting them get too close. If they are carrying bombs they may do some damage.' He drew his flare gun. 'Wait until they are within range, then burn the engines. We'll take one either side, then concentrate on the centre one. Ready?'

The aircraft droned closer, the shadows from their wings black on the rubble beneath them. Ports gaped in the fuselage, and Lanson tightened his lips. Carefully he judged distance, then setting the focus on his flare gun to narrow aperture raised the squat weapon.

Fire lanced from the flared muzzle. Thunder echoed from the ruins at the sound of the discharge, and metal dripped in molten ruin from one of the engine cowlings. Again he fired. Beside him, Bender was behaving as cool as though he were at a shooting gallery.

Above them the planes lurched, lost height, then plunged suddenly to destruction. Flame blossomed from where they hit. Rubble, fragments of the fuselage, scraps of red hot metal, all showered into the air. The concussion threw the two men to the ground and Lanson lay where he had fallen, blood streaming from nose and mouth.

'Are you hurt?' Bender leaned anxiously across the silent figure of his friend.

Lanson grimaced, then spat blood and climbed slowly to his feet. 'Ribs broken,' he muttered. 'I can taste blood, get me to the ship.' He looked at the sky. 'More planes. Hurry!'

Gently Bender carried him into the hangar and up the ladder to the nose. Weakly Lanson slumped into the padded chair, and threw several toggles.

'Ready for take off,' he called. 'Fasten belts.'

'Belts fastened,' replied Bender. He looked anxiously at the tall figure sitting before the controls.

'Coils warm, fuel pumping, prime jets.' Lanson threw switches. From the base of the rocket ship a giant began to mutter, a deep throbbing sound caught and amplified by the metal walls of the hangar. The sound of idling jets.

'Are you all right, Lanson?' Bender leaned across from his position before the astrogator's panel.

'Firing at zero. Three! Two! One. Zero!' The mutter became a roar, a scream of power thundering from the flame spouting rocket jets. Beneath them, the concrete floor of the hangar fused and ran in puddles of molten rock. The ship quivered. Lanson coughed, wiped the back of his hand across his bloodstained lips, and operated the controls.

A giant hand seemed to take hold of the ship. It trembled rose slowly, then at ever increasing speed. Metal snapped and tore as the sharp nose sheered through the thin covering of the hangar roof. Daylight blazed through the ports and Bender had a confused impression of aircraft swinging into bombing position. Then they were accelerating, shooting up to the heavens on a pillar of flame. He was crushed in his seat by the sudden fierce acceleration, and for a moment his senses reeled on the edge of blackout.

Higher they rose. The sky turned black and stars sprang into brilliant life, scattered across the midnight sky like twinkling gems tossed onto a piece of dark velvet. Higher still, and the stars no longer twinkled. They were in space.

Below them the Earth seemed a ball, a strangely mottled ball, the blue of the oceans and the brown of the land mass mingled and distorted by their speed. The sparkling whiteness of the north polar ice cap swung into view beneath them.

'Bender.'

'Yes?'

'Plot the position of the alien space ship. I want an exact time and position equation.'

'What are you going to do?'

Lanson coughed again, then looking at his smeared hand, laughed.

'There's only one thing we can do. The space ship must orbit across the pole. We'll ram down on it as it passes.'

'I see.' Bender bent over the compact computer built into the panel before him. He fed several sets of figures into the machine, tapped a key and read the answer in the display panel.

'The ship will be over the pole in exactly five minutes seven seconds. Plus or minus one tenth of a second error.'

'A tenth of a second! Is that the best you can do?'

'With the information I have, yes.'

'It will have to do. That gives us over five minutes to lose speed and turn.' Lanson laughed again. 'Hold on, Bender. Here we go!'

Flame spouted from the bow tubes. Behind them the gyros whined a shrill protest, and the stars swung sickeningly across the heavens. The ship spun on its short axis, then lost speed as the great main tubes fired along the direction of flight. Slowly they came to a relative stop.

Something flashed below. Something small and round, and moving with incredible speed across the ball of the Earth. The alien space ship!

With a quick gesture, Lanson operated the controls, and behind him, the main driving tubes spouted a mile-long finger of flame. Pressure forced them back into their padded chairs. Before them the ball of the Earth jerked, then began to swell like a balloon. At the highest thrust of rockets designed to escape the gravity of a planet, the space ship lanced through the void towards the alien vessel.

Atmosphere whined about them, heating their heat shield with friction, raising the temperature of the metal almost to melting point. Bender thought of the tanks of fuel behind them, and then lost his worry as he stared through the forward ports.

The small round blob of the alien ship leaped into sudden focus, a gleaming ball, studded with inexplicable mechanisms, and streaking on its path around the Earth. It wasn't small, suddenly it was huge, almost filling the forward vision ports. Abruptly it jerked away.

Steering jets flared from the hull of the attacking ship, and the alien was directly in line again. Even as he stared at the smooth hull of their target, Bender found time to marvel at Lanson's handling of the ship. Beneath his sure touch it answered as easily as a small, light-weight rocket plane.

Again the alien jerked away, and again with deft touches of the controls Lanson brought it back in line with the plunging vessel. Abruptly fire spouted from one of the strange mechanisms. Something reached upwards to the attacking ship, glinting and swirling with menacing life. It touched, crawled over the hull, and then was gone.

Metal screamed, twisted, ran in molten ruin. Fire blossomed about them, filling space with a roaring thunder and glaring light. Something twisted, fell away streaming flame and smoke, a great hole torn in its side. Lanson grunted and tugged at the controls.

Slowly the ship responded. Slowly the

shrieking gyros brought up the nose, lowered the main driving tubes swinging the careering space ship in a loop that could only be measured in hundreds of miles.

'Take the controls, Bender,' Lanson gasped painfully. He coughed again, his mouth filling with blood. 'Set her down in water somewhere, the Great Lakes perhaps, or some sea-coast. Just keep her balanced, watch the levels — ' He slumped in sudden unconsciousness. Grimly, Bender took the controls. It wasn't easy, but landing a space ship could never be easy. Even with his experience of previous landings, Bender sweated over the controls. A blast of the steering jets to compensate for lateral tilt. Another blast to compensate for overcompensation. Gradually the ship lowered itself on a pencil of spouting flame. Water glinted beneath them, a lake. Bender didn't know the name.

When they finally settled with a hiss of steam, he was hardly conscious of the fact. Still he sat, gripping the controls with hands of iron. Gratefully he cut the main drive, blasted the side jets to bring the ship close to the shore, then slumped in sudden fatigue and reaction beside the helpless figure of Lanson.

They were still there when the planes landed. Gentle hands moved them to a camp beside the waters of the lake. Other hands, more skilful, set Lanson's broken ribs, and treated his multiple injuries.

Time passed, and slowly they healed. Bender awoke first, feeling the smart of unguents on his body, and touching the bandages on his head with wondering hands. A face smiled down at him, an old face, lined and worn with care and study.

'Burges!'

'Take it easy,' chuckled the old physicist 'You're in good hands.'

Bender struggled to sit upright 'Lanson?'

'Damaged, but he'll live.' The old face softened as he looked at the silent figure in the next bed. 'We spotted you falling, noticed where you must land, and followed you by plane. Lucky we did. They must have fired some sort of a ray at you. Neither of you had much skin left that was of any use. You'd hit your head sometime during the flight, and had mild concussion.'

'That must have been when we knocked the alien ship off its orbit and into the polar ice field.' Bender frowned. 'The Zytlen?'

'Dead. All of them.'

'Then it's all over?'

'Yes. You are heroes, both of you, and I can get back to my studies again.' He rose and grinned down at the young man. 'Marvin and Slade will be here as soon as they can get away from the city. There is still much to do, and I think that they want you to do it.'

He left, and Bender stared after him through the tent flap. Outside the sun shone and the sound of birds filled the air. Lanson moaned a little, stirring restlessly in his sleep. Bender smiled at him, then stared outside again.

There was still much to do, much to see and to learn. A whole new world waited outside the tent flap. A free world.

We do hope that you have enjoyed reading this large print book.

Did you know that all of our titles are available for purchase?

We publish a wide range of high quality large print books including:
Romances, Mysteries, Classics
General Fiction
Non Fiction and Westerns

Special interest titles available in large print are:
The Little Oxford Dictionary
Music Book, Song Book
Hymn Book, Service Book

Also available from us courtesy of Oxford University Press:
Young Readers' Dictionary
(large print edition)
Young Readers' Thesaurus
(large print edition)

For further information or a free brochure, please contact us at:
Ulverscroft Large Print Books Ltd.,
The Green, Bradgate Road, Anstey,
Leicester, LE7 7FU, England.
Tel: (00 44) **0116 236 4325**
Fax: (00 44) **0116 234 0205**

THE RESURRECTED MAN

E. C. Tubb

After abandoning his ship, space pilot Captain Baron dies in space, his body frozen and perfectly preserved. Five years later, doctors Le Maitre and Whitney, restore him to life using an experimental surgical technique. However, returning to Earth, Baron realises that now being legally dead, his only asset is the novelty of being a Resurrected Man. And, being ruthlessly exploited as such, he commits murder — but Inspector McMillan and his team discover that Baron is no longer quite human . . .